BOONE

Sweet Southern Charmers Book 3

LORI WILDE &
CAROLYN GREENE

"Let me get this straight. You want to advertise for a *dad?*"

The two children, who'd introduced themselves as Bethany and Brad Thomas, gazed up at Boone Shelton, nervous disappointment in their eyes, as if they were afraid that he'd send them home before they accomplished their goal.

Slowly, he rolled up his shirtsleeves. Why were they advertising for a father?

Bethany, the oldest, spoke up. She was around twelve and clearly the ringleader. "Actually, it's for our mom. She can get dates—"

"Yeah, but once they find out about *us*," the boy piped in, hitching a thumb at his scrawny chest, "they don't come back."

The girl nudged her brother with her elbow. "It's not that we're bad," she hastened to reassure Boone. "It's just that Mom wants a man who wants us, too.

And she wants someone *we'd* like. So, this way we'd all be happy."

Boone leaned his back in his chair and propped an elbow on a pile of papers stacked at the front of his desk. When the receptionist had brought the children back here, amusement twinkling in her eyes, and sat them in his office guest chairs, he'd seen their nervousness.

To put them at ease, he'd moved his chair closer to theirs so the desk wouldn't be between them. Now he was beginning to wonder if he should just send them home and tell them to stay out of trouble. But that wasn't his way.

Besides, he was curious.

"So, your mom sent you here to place an ad?"

"Oh, no!" the girl replied. "We thought it up ourselves." She exchanged a look with her brother. "Mom keeps telling us to be proactive, but she isn't doing anything to find someone nice for herself. Or us."

Impressed by their audacity and initiative, Boone spread his arms wide. "But why advertise in the *Bliss Crier*? Why not set her up a profile on a dating site? That makes more sense."

The girl rolled her eyes. "Mom checks our browsing history. She gets weird about stuff like that. Besides, the *Crier* is delivered free to everybody in Bliss, and you've got an online version too, so nobody will miss our ad."

"Boy, will she be surprised when men start coming

out of the woodwork!" The boy rubbed his palms together, and the kids exchanged triumphant smiles.

Boone hated to burst their bubble, but he couldn't allow the types of men who'd be "coming out of the woodwork" to just show up on these nice kids' doorstep. Not only would their mother be displeased, but things could get unpleasant if some weirdo read the wrong message into their ad.

"Look, why don't you talk this over with your mother, and if she says it's okay, come back tomorrow," he said.

"Aw, man!" The boy punched his fist and scowled. "She'll just say no."

From her pocket, the girl pulled out a piece of paper folded to form a makeshift envelope. She opened it and took out two ten-dollar bills and an assortment of coins.

"We've been saving our allowance. We would have had more"—she narrowed her eyes at her brother —"but Brad bought a candy bar yesterday."

Brad seemed unconcerned by his sister's frown. He patted his tummy. "I'm a growing boy."

The girl got up and dumped the money onto Boone's desk. "Is this enough to run the ad for three weeks?"

Twenty-three dollars and forty-five cents wouldn't get them very far, but somehow, he couldn't break that news.

Boone studied the children more closely. They certainly were determined to go through with this.

Their expressions reminded him of the sneaker incident of his youth. When he was a boy, he'd watched a commercial of a kid running so fast he took off flying in the super-powered sneakers, and Boone had been convinced that owning a pair of that brand of sneakers would enable him to run so fast he'd take off and fly, just like the kid on TV.

His mother could have simply told him it was nonsense to think a pair of sneakers would make him fly. Instead, she had let him find out for himself. He'd bugged the neighbors for odd jobs and earned the money for the prized sneakers. When he'd insisted on having a "test flight" in his new shoes, his mother had sought to soften his crash-landing by piling old blankets at the end of the takeoff ramp he'd rigged up in the backyard.

Not only had she cushioned his behind, but she'd cushioned his pride and taught him a valuable lesson, as well.

"Well," she'd said casually as he'd rubbed his sore backside, "it looks like we can't believe everything we see on TV." In his young mind, he'd thought she was every bit as surprised as he was by the disappointing results.

And now these kids thought an ad would bring them all they'd ever wanted. He didn't have the heart to tell them it would bring more of the same kind of men their mother had already met, or that it might be ignored altogether.

Most likely the latter. And in a weekly paper in a

town the size of Bliss, Virginia, the ad would create more curiosity than tangible results.

Boone thought once again of those flying tennis shoes.

"Since you're first-time advertisers with the *Bliss Crier*," he said, returning half the money they'd given him, "you're entitled to the first-timer's discount. But there is one catch."

Both children looked up, suspicion darkening their brown eyes.

"It has to be a blind ad. That means any, uh, *applicants* will write to you in care of this paper. They won't know who you are unless your mother chooses to contact them."

The girl let out her breath. "Good. That way, we can weed out the pervs."

"Well, yeah, to put it bluntly," Boone said.

She blushed. "Sorry. I didn't mean to embarrass you."

Boone grinned. These kids were something else. "So, what do you want the ad to say?"

Bethany cleared her throat. "'Help Wanted: Father. Strong, loving, dependable. Prefer someone as good-looking and as smart as our mother.' Oh, and don't forget, 'Must like kids and animals.'"

They'd obviously rehearsed it. Boone finished jotting it down and turned to Brad. "Is that okay with you?"

"Yeah, but change it to 'Help Wanted: Daddy.'" When his sister shot him a stern look, he explained,

"A father is someone who goes to work, mows the lawn, and punishes you when you're bad. But a daddy is someone who plays ball with you and lets you work on the car with him and takes you for ice cream on Saturday afternoon. That's what I want ... a daddy."

~

While they were in his office, the kids missed their school bus. Boone offered them a ride to their mother's place of business nearby. But first, he made them call her to get permission to ride with him.

He'd been a little surprised that she hadn't asked to speak with him and had given her okay after only a moment's hesitation. When he met her, he planned to take her aside and tell her she should be more careful about who she let those terrific kids ride with.

As he drove, the children chattered excitedly about how many and what kind of people might answer their advertisement.

They pulled into the parking lot at Cordaire Signs, and Boone felt his stomach do its familiar flip-flop at the name.

Nixie Cordaire. The girl who'd grown up two houses away from him. The pretty, petite girl who'd captured his heart and tied his tongue. The problem was, in his adolescent awkwardness, he'd shown his affection by teasing her mercilessly, and she'd never liked him.

Boone hadn't had a chance to look her up since

he'd returned home to Bliss after buying the *Crier* a couple of months ago. He wondered why she didn't have a man in her life. He couldn't imagine anyone overlooking a gem as precious as Nixie Cordaire.

Maybe she wasn't in the office. He hoped. When they did meet again, he wanted to be prepared so he'd say just the right things and didn't fall back on the teasing.

"Thanks for the ride, Mr. Shelton." The kids climbed out of the car and torpedoed into the small building.

Boone followed after them to the back office and found the kids talking excitedly with ... *her.*

He didn't know how it was possible, but she was even more beautiful now than she'd been in high school. She was still petite—still had that same delicate bone structure and graceful way of moving that made him think of a ballerina. Her auburn hair was longer, though, and styled so it emphasized her heart-shaped face ... from wide-set, golden brown eyes to a pointed chin that begged him to cup it in his hand.

She looked up at him and watched him warily.

"Little Nixie Cordaire," he murmured. "Look at you."

Nixie narrowed her eyes. Even after all these years, Boone Shelton was still treating her as if she were his kid sister.

"I've grown up." *In case you haven't noticed,* she added mentally. "And my name's Thomas now."

Boone's eyebrows drew together. "Thomas Cordaire?"

Nixie sighed and fidgeted with her small gold earring. He was doing it again. Deliberately teasing her. It seemed some things never changed.

"Nixie Thomas," she said.

He glanced at her bare hand. "You're divorced?" He couldn't imagine any man being foolish enough to let her get away.

"Widowed."

"I'm sorry." The instant he said it, Boone knew it was a lie. Sorry for the departed Mr. Thomas, sure. But not sorry Nixie was available. He only hoped her husband had deserved her.

"Mom, we decided to find us a daddy," Brad blurted.

"And we're going to find you a husband," Bethany added.

Nixie's startled gaze shot to Boone, then back to the kids. "You did *what?*"

Boone couldn't help himself. The years-old habit hit him as strongly as it had when they were children themselves.

"Oh, come on, Nixie. You don't need to pretend you knew nothing about your kids placing a personals ad for you."

Her eyes widened, and her mouth formed a small O. Boone plunged recklessly ahead.

"If you'd like, I could go through my phone book and fix you up with someone nice."

"Really?" said Bethany and Brad in unison.

"Of course not," Nixie admonished. Then her tone softened. "He was just kidding."

She looked askance at Boone as if to double-check that he *had* been joking.

"Why don't you two tell me what you were doing at the newspaper office?"

After they gave their scrambled version of what had transpired, and Boone had offered his two cents' worth, Nixie turned to him, one hand on her jeans-clad hip.

"Boone! How could you?" She tossed her hair with one hand, as she'd always done when perturbed with him. "It's one thing to involve me in your corny teasing, but to drag two little kids into your silly prank...."

"I'm not little," Brad insisted. He pushed up his sleeve and flexed his wiry arm to display a puny muscle. "See."

Boone picked the boy up and tucked him under one arm as casually as a businessman carries a newspaper. Brad giggled at the unexpected action.

"It's not what you think," said Boone.

"How could you allow—even encourage—the children to proceed with such an ad?"

"Sometimes," Boone began, "it's best to let kids find out for themselves that super-power sneakers won't make you fly."

LORI WILDE & & CAROLYN GREENE

"What?"

Even Bethany, who was doodling on a pad of paper at her mother's desk, stopped and waited for his explanation.

"What I'm trying to say is that if I hadn't let them place the ad, they would've been disappointed, and it would've squelched their initiative."

By now, Brad, still dangling under Boone's arm, was moving his arms and legs in a slow swimming motion.

"Aw, c'mon, Mom. Be a sport."

Nixie rolled her eyes. She could tell it would be impossible to make Boone see how foolish such a scheme was.

"It's a blind ad," Boone assured her, "so no one will know it's you. Besides, there probably won't be many responses."

The kids were waiting expectantly for her answer.

She worried that they might be disappointed when their plan failed. But they would be disappointed if she said no after all their effort. Still, Nixie wasn't happy about being pushed into a corner.

Finally, reluctantly, she agreed to let them pursue this crazy plan.

"All *right*," said Brad from his airborne position.

Bethany beamed.

Boone smiled. "It might be fun. And who knows, you may find the man of your dreams."

Nixie had a sickening feeling that this man of her nightmares held her love life in his brawny hands.

2

Boone tugged at the frilly pink dress that had ridden up around his waist. Under his stiff khaki pants, the pantyhose bagged around his knees and ankles. He resisted the urge to pull them up.

Across the road at the elementary school, Cub Scouts and their parents gathered at the front door, waiting for someone to unlock it. He hated being late, especially when Scouts were depending on him. And even more so, when he'd talked Nixie into bringing Brad to watch the Cub Scout play rehearsal tonight. Maybe the kid would enjoy the camaraderie enough to join the pack.

Boone patted his overcoat pocket to check for the key and sprinted across the road.

Too late, he saw the blue sedan round the corner without slowing down. With the skill of a lifelong athlete, he leaped to avoid a direct impact. His body glanced off the front fender, then connected solidly with the hard pavement.

His world went black.

Talk about being in the right place at the right time.

Nixie had stopped at the rescue squad building to check the training schedule before heading home, and that was when the call came in about a hit-and-run accident.

Another had volunteer arrived while she was pulling on her jumpsuit. In a few seconds, they were on the road with sirens blaring.

This time the victim was lucky. Jeff pulled the ambulance up at the accident site just four minutes after they received the call. Nixie hoped this kind of luck would hold out until they could recruit and train more volunteers.

Jumping lightly down from the cab of the ambulance, she grabbed her bag and trotted back to where a dozen little boys in blue uniforms and neckerchiefs gathered around a man in an overcoat.

"Excuse me, coming through."

Kneeling beside the unconscious form, she checked his pulse and respiration. Both were steady and strong.

Nixie touched the man's cheek, and her breath caught in her throat. The blond-haired giant she tended was none other than Boone Shelton.

Briefly, she wondered if this was another elaborate setup for a joke at her expense. Fortunately, her paranoia left as quickly as it came. Boone would never joke about something as serious as this.

She took another look at his massive body lying so still on the pavement, and it scared her. She'd never seen him so helpless and vulnerable before. Boone had always been the protector, never the protected.

Nixie became aware of Jeff moving the crowd back, and she turned her attention to the lump on Boone's forehead. She had to stay busy—partly to help Boone and partly to keep from reacting emotionally to the fact that the boy she'd grown up with was lying helpless before her and needed her more now than he ever had.

He appeared to have some slight road rash on his hands and across his cheek, but the lump—and his unconsciousness—was what concerned her most. She pushed the shaggy blond hair off his forehead to closer examine the injury.

Boone winced, and his eyelashes fluttered before they opened and focused on Nixie. "Well," he murmured, "if it isn't little Nixie Cordaire. Still taking care of people, aren't you?"

Nixie let out a big breath she hadn't realized she'd been holding. "Boone? What are you doing here?"

Boone cautiously glanced around him. "Presently? Lying in the middle of the road."

Jeff knelt beside her. "How is he? Should I call for the chopper?"

"No, I don't think that'll be necessary. Why don't you get the gurney while I check for fractures?" Turning to Boone, she said, "Let me know if it hurts."

"You'll be the second to know."

Aware of those pale-blue eyes watching her every move, Nixie felt almost shy as she ran her hands over his neck, shoulders, arms, and legs.

Just pretend he's the dummy you worked on in training class.

But there was no way she could mistake his overdeveloped frame for a training dummy. Moving her hands to his abdomen, she pressed lightly to check for obvious internal injuries. He showed no sign of pain.

"If you're finished poking me," Boone said, attempting to rise, "those Cub Scouts are waiting for me. *Ohhh*." He pressed a hand to his head and leaned back on one elbow.

"Don't try to get up. You took quite a whack to your forehead. You ought to let a doctor look at that."

"What about the dress rehearsal?" one of the mothers asked.

Boone fished a key out of his coat pocket and tossed it to the woman. "Go on without me. I'll be back in an hour."

Nixie gave a delicate snort. "When's the last time you've been to an emergency room?"

It was a good thing Boone had regained consciousness because Nixie doubted whether she and Jeff and all of the Cub Scouts together could have lifted him into the ambulance. Well over six feet tall, the massive physique that had been easy to distinguish on the high school football field was now even broader than it had been fifteen years ago.

"What do you weigh these days, two thirty?" she asked after he lay down in the back of the ambulance.

"No, I'm kinda puny now. Down to two eighteen."

"Puny" was hardly the word to describe Boone Shelton. His chest seemed big enough to land an airplane on, and his arms bulged against the sleeves of his overcoat.

Odd, but why would he be wearing an overcoat on such a balmy spring day as this? She adjusted the straps that secured him to the gurney and signaled Jeff to begin the drive to the hospital.

"This is a first for me," said Boone.

"Riding in an ambulance?"

"Being tied to the bed by a beautiful woman."

There had once been a day when his teasing would have reduced her to blushing and stammering. Fifteen years, one marriage, and two kids later, she didn't blush so easily. But she would have stammered if she hadn't clamped down on the inside of her bottom lip.

"No blushing? What happened to the pink cheeks Nixie Cordaire was always famous for?"

Nixie squirmed on the padded bench beside him.

Why was it that, even though he was reclining, he seemed to tower over her?

Nixie busied herself by inspecting his forehead, determinedly ignoring the butterflies fluttering around in her stomach.

"You must be burning up in that overcoat. Let me help you."

"No—"

Before he could stop her, Nixie unfastened the top button. Boone's big hands closed around hers, but she already had two buttons undone.

Her eyes widened, and her jaw dropped, and her fingers stilled. *Holy moly, what was this?*

Pink ruffles and white lace spilled from the vee of his coat. Dusty-blond chest hairs sprang from the frilly neckline. She'd seen stranger sights during her years as a volunteer rescue worker, but never had she been more surprised than now. Why in heaven's name was he wearing a ballet tutu?

Dragging her eyes away from the froufrou, she met Boone's gaze.

"Blue is more your color," she said, immensely pleased to have caught him with his pants down, so to speak.

If she didn't know better, she would have sworn Boone Shelton blushed. "I was on my way to a dress rehearsal for the Cub Scout play. Remember?"

Nixie gave up all hope of keeping the humor out of her expression. She raised one eyebrow. "What play is that?"

"I play the part of ... Dorothy," he said.

This was too much.

"Right," she retorted, "and all those Cub Scouts are munchkins."

"It's not *that* play."

This was too much, it was all she could do not to burst out laughing. Of course, she believed him. He would have better taste than to wear that awful tutu for kicks. But after all those years of putting up with his endless teasing, she could finally get even. She couldn't pass up this opportunity.

"Listen, I know a couple of really nice guys. Maybe we could, like, double-date sometime."

"Yeah, yeah, really funny."

"Come over to my place, and I'll show you how to shave your legs."

The ambulance pulled to a stop at the hospital's entrance. While Nixie unbuckled her seat belt, Boone refastened the top buttons of his coat.

Nixie released the gurney for Jeff, and Boone fumbled with the restraints that held him down. "I can walk."

"Nope, you're on the gurney, protocol," Jeff said.

Once inside the hospital, Boone persuaded them to let him transfer into the wheelchair, and they pushed him to the ER nurse.

"Got a live one this evening, Virginia." Nixie winked at the head nurse. "This is 'Dorothy,' who *claims* he was on his way to a dress rehearsal play."

The woman quickly sized him up and burst out

laughing. "Hello, Dorothy! What seems to be your problem?"

Boone shot Nixie a look of grudging admiration for zinging him with the kind of teasing he'd dished out to her over the years. Since the emergency room was unusually slow tonight, Boone was processed, examined, and x-rayed quickly.

Nixie told Jeff to take the ambulance back to the station. Then she called Uncle Jay to ask him to bring over one of his shirts and a pair of jeans. Uncle Jay was about Boone's size, but he was proportioned differently.

Her uncle assured her that Aunt Lauren would give the children supper and tried to ferret out the reason for the shirt and jeans.

"It's for a friend," Nixie said, hoping he wouldn't ask too many questions. Lying wasn't one of her strong points, and even though she'd taken delight in serving Boone his own brand of teasing, she didn't wish to get her uncle involved in the joke. "He was in an accident," she added, hoping Uncle Jay would assume that Boone's shirt had been bloodied or torn.

By the time her uncle arrived, Boone was ready to be released. Fortunately, he didn't have a concussion —just a goose egg over his left eyebrow. After a brief reintroduction to Jay, he gratefully accepted the shirt and pants.

He tugged on the shirt.

Nixie noticed how his thick arms stretched against the short sleeves. Although buttons strained across the chest, the fabric fell lax over his trim abdomen. If the sight of his arms could undo her like this, she needed to get out of the room pronto before he shimmied into those jeans.

Virginia called out, "Hey, Dorothy, don't forget your dress." She held up a large paper bag.

Uncle Jay's eyebrows shot up when Boone went back to retrieve the bag. "Dorothy?"

"Uh, let me carry that for you, Boone," Nixie offered. "And we'll leave you to put your pants on."

Uncle Jay followed Nixie to the nurse's desk while Boone finished dressing in the curtained ER cubicle. He eyed the bag she'd practically yanked from Boone's hand. "A *dress?*"

"Uncle Jay, please don't start."

"Oh, don't worry about him," Virginia reassured with a wave of her hand. "I'm sure his toes point the right way in a bathroom stall. He was wearing boxers under his leggings."

Boone strolled from behind the curtain, fully clothed and grinning. It seemed he was enjoying the notoriety.

In the waiting room, an elderly woman pursed her lips and glared at him.

"You've changed a lot since we last saw you," her uncle said. Then he started to laugh, his ample stomach bouncing in rhythm to his hearty chuckles.

Boone laid a hand on the older man's shoulder as he and Nixie followed him out to the car. "And you haven't, Mr. Cordaire. Not one little bit."

"And after Uncle Jay learned about the dress, he was like a pit bull with a meaty bone. He wouldn't let go," Nixie told her aunt.

"That's my Jay." Lauren smiled.

"He offered to stop at the pharmacy on the way to Boone's house so he could pick up cosmetics and leggings."

"Sounds like a fun time." Aunt Lauren giggled.

"Then Uncle Jay asked Boone whether he preferred to wear front or back-hook bras." Nixie took a handful of popcorn, then passed the bowl to her daughter.

"How did Boone take it?"

"You know Boone. He was a good sport and dished it right back, but I was beginning to feel uncomfortable for him."

"So, you still have feelings for him." Aunt Lauren's statement was more of an observation than a question.

Nixie shook her head. Her aunt and uncle had been like second parents to her since her father's job had taken her parents away from the East Coast just months before Paul died.

In his own irrepressible way, Uncle Jay had sought to lighten her spirits with teasing and practical jokes. In the process, his infectious humor had shaped eight-year-old Brad into a relentless prankster who frequently made eleven-year-old Bethany the victim of his mischief.

Aunt Lauren, on the other hand, had provided a calm and steadying influence for Nixie and the children.

In the past eight years, since Paul's death, hers had been the shoulders Nixie cried upon and leaned on. As well as being a pillar of strength for Nixie, Aunt Lauren was also the unwanted matchmaker in her life. Nixie considered the possibility that her aunt was now pointing a Cupid's arrow at her high school nemesis.

"The only feeling I ever had for Boone Shelton was dread of being in the same room with him. He couldn't stand me, and he let me know it by constantly picking on me."

Lauren bestowed a loving smile on her husband, who had assumed his regular Friday night position in the wide recliner where he streamed movies. Bethany and Brad, perched on the padded chair arms, cuddled against their great-uncle and ate popcorn out of the bowl balanced on his stomach.

"Your Uncle Jay used to pull my hair," Aunt Lauren said. "That's how I knew he was interested in me."

Jay looked up from the TV and grunted. "Your hair looked too thick and pretty to be real. I was just checking to see if it was a wig."

The children giggled.

"Even if that was why he picked on me, which I

doubt," said Nixie, "it wouldn't work. Boone's not my type."

"Why not?" asked Bethany, who was starting to take an interest in the opposite sex.

"Because," Nixie said, trying vainly to put into words why she was opposed to a relationship with Boone. For lack of a better explanation, she said, "He's a jock."

"So?"

"So, she's saying," Uncle Jay piped in, "she'd rather have a couch potato like me."

"What kind of man are you looking for?" Aunt Lauren prodded.

Nixie thought a moment and gave a little sigh before answering. "I want a man who reads and can carry on a discussion about a good book. My wish list is for someone who's intelligent and sensitive to other people's needs. And, of course, someone who would be a good father for Bethany and Brad."

Aunt Lauren patted Nixie's arm. "Honey, you're not going to find another Paul. You ought to widen your horizons a little. Besides, that very well could describe Boone Shelton. He has a lot going for him, and he's a successful businessman, what with being the new owner of the *Bliss Crier*."

"Anyone can buy and manage a small newspaper." She wondered if taking over the newspaper was all that had brought him back to his hometown. In a moment of peevishness, Nixie doubted he'd last more than six months with the print news dying quicker than a cactus in Alaska.

Aunt Lauren peered through the top of her reading glasses at Nixie. "Just as anyone can buy and manage a sign shop?"

Zing! Her aunt had ever so gently put her in her place. Paul had helped her buy the sign shop. Although it had been a healthy business when she'd bought it, it had nevertheless been a trial, not only to learn the system but to make the business grow. It had been a mental and physical challenge to make Cordaire Signs run like a well-oiled machine.

"Touché."

"Mom," Bethany interrupted, "Brad said he left Tarzan's cage open so the bird could chase my cat."

Brad smiled as if proud that he'd managed to goad his sister yet again. To make matters worse, Uncle Jay was doing a poor job of hiding his amusement at the sibling squabble.

The movie was over, and it was time to go home, anyway. "Come on, let's go see if Tarzan is terrorizing the cat."

Nixie hugged her aunt and uncle good night while Bethany sprinted across the lawn to their house next door.

When they entered the spacious tri-level home, everything seemed to be in order. She soon located a safe and purring Precious. Knowing the parrot's favorite pastime, Nixie checked the Venetian blind cords to see if Tarzan was swinging on them. No sign of the feathered trapeze artist anywhere.

She found Brad in front of the cage that held its own special place in the living room. He was grinning devilishly. "I must've made a mistake," he said. "Tarzan's all locked up, nice and tight."

"Mom, he knew it all along. You've got to do something about that little...." Bethany ranted on with a tirade of complaints about her little brother.

Nixie tuned out her daughter but continued thinking about what Bethany had said. She would have to do something about Brad's antics. His pranks were becoming more frequent. None had been malicious, but they were growing in severity.

Her uncle's encouragement hadn't helped. Nixie recalled with a shudder the time she'd found fake vomit in her shoe. Brad had borrowed the prop from Uncle Jay's "gag bag." Yes, she definitely had to do something about her son. But what? She suspected that what he needed was a man's firm guidance. A man other than Uncle Jay, that was.

Remembering her aunt's matchmaking comments, Nixie knew she'd need a better reason than Brad's discipline to get involved with a man.

3

With her hair caught up in a bandana, Nixie was stripping bedsheets, and the children were performing their Saturday morning chores when the doorbell rang.

"Close the door. Tarzan's loose," Brad shouted.

Nixie opened the door to find Boone on her front porch.

Wearing a teal Henley shirt with the sleeves cut out and jeans that were sliced at the knees and frayed on the thighs, he looked like the most scrumptious vagabond she'd ever seen. She was glad to see the lump on his forehead was almost gone. Only a pink scrape remained.

"The scarf is a nice touch," he said.

Suddenly self-conscious, Nixie touched a hand to the bandana. Why did he make her feel like an insecure teenager?

"Mom! Tarzan!"

Remembering the parrot, Nixie grabbed Boone's elbow and pulled him into the foyer.

"I didn't realize you'd be so glad to see me." He glanced pointedly at his elbow where her hand still rested.

Hurriedly slamming the door shut behind him, she said, "The bird is out."

"I beg your pardon?"

A raucous jungle yell reverberated from the living room. Boone startled and stepped back. "What the heck?"

"Oh, that's just Tarzan," she explained. "He's swinging on his vine."

Boone stared at the woman who was even more beautiful now than she had been at sixteen. That was the last time he'd seen her before going off to college and to make his mark in the world.

"Won't you come in?" Nixie led him to the living room, where Brad dusted the television set, and Bethany picked up back copies of the *Bliss Crier* and stacked them in a bin; a yellow cat cowered under the couch, and a green-and-red bird dangled at the end of a Venetian blind cord, its wings flapping almost in rhythm to a popular tune blaring from the radio.

"Hi," said Bethany. "Welcome to our zoo."

Brad dropped his dust rag. "Did anybody answer our ad?"

Nixie shot them both a quelling look.

Boone grabbed the boy and pretended to punch him in the stomach. "Not yet, sport. The ad only came out today."

He let go of the laughing boy and turned to Nixie.

"I didn't mean to interrupt your chores. I stopped next door to return your uncle's shirt." Boone withdrew three tickets from his pocket and handed them to Nixie. "And to bring these to you. They're tickets to the Cub Scout play tonight. Your aunt and uncle said they'd be there." He watched the wariness skitter across her delicate features. "I hope you can come, too."

"Are you going to wear that pink dress Uncle Jay told us about?" asked Brad.

Boone rumpled the boy's blond hair. "Sure, and if you want, you can try it on after the play."

"No way, José."

"Boone, if this is payment for our rescue and taxi services yesterday, a donation to the squad would be more beneficial."

He hadn't intended the tickets as payment for her help. He'd merely wanted her seated in the audience. He wanted her to be his good luck charm again.

Every time the dark-haired lovely had accompanied his sister to the school football games, Bliss High had taken the trophy. Boone remembered scanning the crowd for her face and playing his best after he'd found her. If only he'd been able to tell her how much her presence had meant to him. Or how much it had hurt when she'd brought a date.

But, even if he'd been able to express his feelings, she wouldn't have given him a second glance. Phoenix Cordaire had been pretty and popular. She was known for being a giver and spent much of her spare time tutoring others, visiting at the nursing home, and helping organize the annual local walkathon for spina bifida.

Boone, on the other hand, was known as "Boone the Goon," the jock who was involved in every sport from football to wrestling. He'd been convinced she'd never give him a second look. Maybe his relentless teasing had been a subconscious effort to push her away before she had the chance to reject him.

"I'll send a check next week, but I still want you to come tonight." She hesitated, so he decided to play dirty. "I'm sure Bethany and Brad would like to see it, especially since they missed the rehearsal last night. Wouldn't you, kids?"

"Say yes, Mom. It sounds like fun," Bethany pleaded.

Brad was more direct. "Yeah, I want to see Mr. Shelton dressed like a girl."

A buzzer blared in another room. Nixie seized the opportunity to leave the room and collect her thoughts before answering. She wasn't sure she was ready for the feelings that surfaced whenever she was around him. "Excuse me a minute," she said and headed for the stairs. "My washing machine's off-balance."

Bethany waited until her mother had left the room and directed a meaningful look at her brother. "That's not the only thing around here that's off-balance."

Boone sat down on the couch and was startled when the forgotten parrot demanded behind him, "Did you brush your teeth?"

Preparing to scold the bird, Brad shook his finger at it. Tarzan beat him to the punch and yelled, "Shut up, stupid!"

The boy seemed surprised, but he quickly covered his embarrassment by admonishing, "You're supposed to be on my side." Then, in explanation, he added, "Tarzan came to us with a lot of bad habits."

The bird flew across the room and landed on top of the wall clock. "Cuckoo," said Tarzan.

Bethany giggled and told the bird, "I'm sure Mr. Shelton knows that already."

Boone laughed out loud, and the parrot followed with a giggle that sounded remarkably like Bethany's.

"How old are you?" Boone asked the girl. He was amazed that, even though her hair was honey-colored instead of auburn, she looked so much like her mother.

Brad answered for his sister. "Mom said she's eleven, going on forty."

"Hmm," said Boone. "That's even older than me." He liked the kids, probably because their spirit reminded him of Nixie. Despite their contrary comments, he could tell they really liked each other. Maybe he could recruit the boy into his Scout pack. With a lot of rationalizing, he could even convince himself that his motives for doing so were purely altruistic.

He listened patiently while Brad described a martial art technique he'd seen on a television cartoon.

Downstairs in the utility room, Nixie deliberately dawdled with the laundry while her kids raked this latest male visitor over the coals. They weren't bad children, but their high-spirited antics had been known to chase away more than one gentleman guest. She considered them her human litmus test. She'd even cross-stitched a pillow that indicated her opinion on the matter. *Love Me, Love My Kids.*

Nixie had restarted the washer and was going up the steps when she heard Brad yell, "*Hiii-yah!*" Immediately after, Boone's voice rang out, and Nixie heard a loud thump. Uncertain what her son had done this time, she ran to the living room.

Boone lay flat on his back, and Brad's eyes were wide with excitement. "I flipped him, Mom. All by myself!"

Bethany rolled her eyes. "Brad, you're such a dork sometimes. Couldn't you tell he *let* you do it?"

Boone grinned, the action reminding Nixie of the many times he'd looked at her in just that way before delivering a verbal gibe.

"Are you all right?" she asked.

He rose from the floor and stood in front of her in a fluid motion not normally expected from a man with his bulk. "I'm fine. We were just horsing around."

"Mom doesn't let us horse around in the living room," Bethany announced.

His eyes never leaving Nixie's, he asked, "Does she allow it in the bedroom?"

"Sometimes," said Brad, "if we don't play too rough."

He grinned at Nixie. "Oh, I don't believe in playing too rough in the bedroom, either."

Nixie swallowed. She wasn't sure whether it was the way he pinned her with his gaze or the double entendre of his words, but either way, she was feeling quite warm. She had always been the loser in their verbal wrestling matches. She dared not speculate about a bedroom wrestling match, no matter how intriguing the idea.

"Be ready at six thirty," he said, moving toward the door.

She was ready now.

She ran a hand across her brow and brushed aside the wispy fringes that had suddenly grown damp.

"I want us to get there early so Brad can watch the backstage goings-on before the play."

Nixie abruptly came back to reality and followed Boone outside. He flashed her a smile and jogged across the yard on the footworn path between her house and her aunt's and uncle's, where his car was parked. She couldn't help admiring how the shirt emphasized the broadness of his back or the way those tattered jeans clung like a second skin to his muscular buns and thighs.

He was in his car and gone before she remembered she hadn't agreed to attend the play.

Tonight was bingo night at the squad building. It was also Nixie's turn to call the numbers, but another volunteer had agreed to fill in for her.

While the kids bickered about whose turn it was to clear the dinner table, Nixie concentrated on making herself look perfect. Whenever she was feeling less than composed inwardly, she took extra pains with her outward appearance to help bolster her confidence.

She kept the jewelry simple so she wouldn't look out of place at the gathering of Cub Scouts and their families. The tulip-shaped yellow-and-black dress accentuated the curve of her waist and hips, stopping at a flattering level just above the knee. She wished she had more curve for the top part of the dress but quickly rejected the urge to fill that area by other means. Even so, she'd achieved the effect she wanted. Being flawless on the outside helped cover a multitude of cracks in the armor underneath.

When Boone arrived at the Thomas home for the

second time that day, he was presented with a sight so breathtaking all he could do was stare. Gone were the jeans, sweatshirt, and scarf. She was the girl of his dreams, only much more grown-up. He let his eyes drink in the sight of her, committing the picture to memory.

He wanted to tell her how stunning she looked. How the light floral scent of her perfume taunted him and made him want to kiss her until those doe-like golden-brown eyes closed from the pleasure of it. But he didn't know how to put those impressions into words. Instead, he reverted to his past behavior and changed the subject.

"Are Brad and Bethany ready?"

Nixie blinked. She'd been caught up in the intensity of his gaze, immobilized like a deer dazzled by headlights. Then, abruptly, his words had brought her out of the spell as surely as if he'd snapped his fingers.

Perhaps she had imagined the strange force that had seemed to pass between them. As Bethany would say, she needed to take a reality check.

At the elementary school, the reality was that Boone Shelton was quite popular with the children. The young boys flocked around him, begging to see how many he could lift with one arm. With three of the smaller children dangling from his flexed limb and two clinging to his back, he caught Nixie's eye and grinned. "It's one way to keep fit."

Nixie smiled back. Most men who'd been as large as Boone had been in his teens would have become soft and overweight by their thirties. But not Boone. He put too much stock in his body to let it lose its tone. Nixie remembered the exuberance with which he had thrown himself into high school sports. With his superior build and single-minded determination, he became the star of every athletic event he entered.

As the boys' excitement level rose, so did their volume, but Boone easily brought them under control with a quiet admonishment and set each to a particular task. Nixie was pleased at how smoothly he involved Brad with the rest of the boys and solicited Bethany's help in arranging the props onstage. No child was favored over another, but each was made to feel special.

Even Nixie was made to feel useful, handing out photocopies of the typed script and coaching the youngsters on their lines. She was engrossed in helping one forgetful youngster when a wave of giggles swept through the classroom where they had assembled.

Looking up, she saw Boone in that notorious pink dress. With a neck like a tree stump, broad shoulders, hairy arms, narrow hips, and thick legs, he looked anything but girly.

The tacky red wig that sat askew on his head seemed incongruous with the hard, chiseled lines of his face and faint shadow of beard on his jaw. The stuffing in the front of the dress had migrated to form two asymmetrical lumps. And the white leggings he had put on—and managed to run—clearly defined the flattened curls of leg hair that liberally covered his shins and calves. Large-size sneakers finished the ensemble.

"Look," exclaimed Brad, "it's Boone Hilda!"

The room exploded with good-natured laughter.

A scowl grew on Boone's face. It was a look that could make a street gang member tremble in his shoes. Walking slowly and deliberately to Brad, he clasped the boy under each arm, lifted him to eye level, and gave him a stern glare.

The room grew deadly silent, and all eyes turned to stare at the pack leader and the new kid. Brad's expression was a mixture of confusion, fear, and curiosity.

Bethany timidly tugged the lace ruffle at Boone's elbow. "He didn't mean it, Mr. Shelton. He was just kidding."

Nixie opened her mouth to demand that he put her son down, but he spoke first, his voice deep and menacing.

"The name is Dorothy," he growled at the boy. "Dorothy Priscilla Lillywhite." For emphasis, he gave Brad a gentle shake. "And *don't* you forget it!"

Brad's face split into a broad smile. The rest of the boys gathered around the pink giant, clamoring, "Scare me, Boone, scare me."

Nixie slowly let out her breath. From the time she was seven—when the Sheltons had moved to Bliss—until she was sixteen and Boone moved away from home, she had never seen or heard of him using his size to bully or intimidate anyone. She knew he'd never harm or even frighten anyone intentionally. Nixie chalked up her reaction to a mother's protective instincts.

"Did you see that, Mom?" Brad's face was flush with excitement. "He almost scared the pudding out of me!"

"Me, too." That was at least partly true.

Boone disengaged himself from the tangle of boys who swarmed around him like gnats. He crossed to where Nixie stood with her family and, after playboxing with Brad, draped his arms around the shoulders of both Bethany and Nixie.

"It's almost time for the show to start. I've reserved front row seats for you ladies. And your aunt and uncle." With a light tug of Bethany's hair, he added, "I expect you to lead the applause for us."

Bethany blushed under his flirting wink, reminding Nixie of the many occasions on which he'd made her blush and then teased her about her pink cheeks. "What about Brad?" the girl asked.

"If he'd like, he can help out backstage and watch the play from there."

Judging from her son's reaction, she would have thought he'd been invited by the president to have dinner at the White House. She gave her consent after making the boy promise not to touch anything unless specifically instructed. Boone flashed her a questioning glance but remained silent.

Uncle Jay and Aunt Lauren waited for them in the

front row. The play was much more entertaining than Nixie had anticipated. From missed cues to forgotten lines to dropped props, the boys happily fumbled their way through their parts. They actually seemed to enjoy the hysterical laughter coming from the audience. Occasionally, Nixie and her family could see Brad, offstage, helping a boy change costumes or handing another his prop.

"Look, Mom," whispered Bethany, "Brad's not playing tricks on anyone."

Nixie crossed her fingers and, satisfied that her son would behave himself, focused her attention on Boone. Although his entrance had been met with swells of laughter, he seemed perfectly at ease playing the part of a young girl who had moved to a new neighborhood and was shunned by the previously all-boy residents.

Despite his comical appearance, Boone played the part with great sensitivity. He was so convincing that the Scout who was Dorothy's main tormentor actually apologized for being so mean. Action stopped for a moment while Boone reassured the boy and whispered instructions so he could pick up in the script where he'd left off.

Nixie was amazed that, no matter who forgot a part, Boone was able to prompt the child with the correct line. He must have memorized the entire script.

The play ended shortly after Boone, still acting the part of Dorothy, came onstage with a BMX bike and performed a series of awesome stunts. Even in a dress, his was an incredible body to watch.

For their parts, the Cub Scouts didn't have to act out their amazement at Boone's performance. The emotion was genuine. Nine mouths gaped open at once.

When Nixie realized her expression matched the boys', she snapped her jaw shut. A familiar feeling swept over her, and she recognized it as the same one she'd felt every time Boone had scored a touchdown or pinned a wrestling opponent to the mat.

Back then, she'd considered her possessive pride in his achievements to be related to her connection with him via his sister. Since she and Ellen had been close, Nixie had been happy for him in his accomplishments, just as she would for a brother ... sort of.

The play ended with the boys befriending the girl and Dorothy offering to teach them some of her stunts.

The curtains closed, and Nixie was left with a warm, comfortable glow deep inside. She attributed the feeling to the production's happy ending, but honesty forced her to admit, even if only a little bit, that her reaction was much more personal than that.

"Wasn't he terrific?" said Aunt Lauren.

"Yes," Nixie agreed. "I couldn't get over how well he played his part."

"Played his part? I was talking about what a terrific job Brad did handing the actors their props and closing the curtains at the right time."

Nixie faltered. Of course Aunt Lauren had been talking about Brad's ability to concentrate on his assignment and do a good job of it. Nixie had been so enthralled with Boone that she'd forgotten to look at her own son.

Aunt Lauren watched her with undisguised speculation. Embarrassed by her *faux pas*, Nixie groped under the seat for her purse. Finding it, she stood and led her family backstage before Aunt Lauren started with any probing questions.

The hall leading backstage was crowded with parents and well-wishers. After the crowd thinned and they congratulated Brad on his role as stagehand, Boone broke away from another group and came over to join them.

"Weren't these boys great?"

"They were wonderful." Nixie couldn't help adding, "And you were very believable as Dorothy."

He'd changed out of his costume but easily slipped back into his role. He slanted a saucy grin at Nixie. "A girl does what a girl has to do."

Nixie decided that he was one of the most unique men she'd ever known. So secure was he in his own masculinity, he was comfortable donning a dress for the Cub Scout play and even joking about it. She felt certain that should someone try to goad him about his part, he would refuse to take offense.

Come to think of it, he'd been much the same way in high school. Despite the energy and enthusiasm he had poured into sports, he hadn't seemed to care what others thought of his athletic accomplishments. If he had fumbled a ball and was chided about it, he'd shrug and say, "I missed. So what?" He had been equally blasé about praise he'd received for pushing his team to victory. Whereas the attention might have unsettled other boys during those traumatic teen years, Boone had seemed unaffected by it all.

One fringe benefit of being the star player was that he never lacked for a date with a pretty girl. But he was even low-key about that. More than one of Nixie's friends who had been interested in him—but too shy to let him know it—remarked how lucky she was to see him almost every day. *Right,* Nixie had thought at the time, *I'm so lucky to have him torture me every time I visit his sister.*

An hour later, after the Scouts had cleaned the school auditorium and her aunt and uncle had taken Nixie's children home, Boone locked the school door and led her to his car in the rear parking lot. The car, like its owner, was big yet understated. A quality machine, but not flashy.

The night was cool. There were no clouds to hold the day's warmth close to the earth. Stars glimmered brightly, competing with the moon for top billing, and the blinking lights of an aircraft passed high overhead.

Boone slowly walked past the sole car in the parking lot toward the fence that enclosed the football field. He seemed remote, as if in a trance.

Nixie walked up behind him. Her eyes followed his to the muddy playing field. She remembered the times he had played in conditions such as this. No matter how many layers of mud he'd worn, she'd never had any difficulty spotting him. And no matter how ruthlessly he'd teased her—even on the day of the game—she'd always cheered him on from the stands.

Boone broke the silence. "Sure brings back memories."

From the tone of voice, Nixie knew that even though he'd pretended only a mild interest in the game, it had meant much more. It had been as if much more than winning or losing a game had been riding on how well he played.

He opened the gate and waited for her to step through. They walked together in silence. When they reached the bleachers, Nixie sat primly on the lowest bench and hugged her arms.

He was used to seeing her near the top row, giggling with his sister. Her movements, though more refined with practice and the confidence that came from growing older, were the same, however. *Yes, indeed,* he thought, *it sure brought back memories.*

Boone jerked his thoughts back to the present. If he didn't keep his mind on target, he'd forget the reason he'd asked to speak to her tonight. Quickly, before his mind wandered back to the way her hair shone in the moonlight, he described Brad's interest in joining the Scouts and the benefits of membership. He was surprised when she resisted the suggestion.

After all Scouting had done for him—helping him grow from the shy, awkward new kid in the community to someone confident in his own abilities—he couldn't imagine anyone turning down the opportunity for her child to join. Unless, of course, she had problems getting him to the weekly den meetings.

"If transportation is a problem, I'll be glad to give him a ride."

Nixie paused before answering. She wondered how to explain the protectiveness she felt toward her son—her baby. Unless someone had been through what she had with Brad, she doubted he would understand the tight bonds she felt for him. Uncle Jay had called those bonds apron strings, but she couldn't bear to think of anything bad happening to her child after all he'd been through already.

"The transportation isn't a problem. I just ... don't think it's safe to let him do some of the risky activities that are required."

"*Risky* activities?"

Nixie stiffened, preparing to be ridiculed yet again for her protectiveness. Or, as Uncle Jay called it, "overprotectiveness."

"Yes. I consider camping, woodworking, rough sports—that kind of thing—too risky for Brad."

She was glad she couldn't discern his expression,

for she was sure he thought her silly, just as everyone else did.

Instead of ridiculing her, however, he started describing the activities and ways in which the leaders safeguarded against injury. She could see he wouldn't let up until he had convinced her Brad would be safe in his care ... or until she explained why she still couldn't take the chance.

"Brad was born after a difficult delivery. The doctor didn't think he was going to make it, but the little rascal pulled through, anyway." Even now, it still amazed her that he'd ever made it through those first few days. "Just when we thought the crisis was over, he stopped breathing in his sleep. The first few times, Paul was there to help me revive him. Then after Paul died, it was up to me to go to Brad every time the monitor alarm went off. I guess you could say he has 'died' a half dozen times already."

Nixie fought to still the trembling that had little to do with the evening's chill.

"As a rescue volunteer, I've seen enough victims to know that no activity is completely safe," she said. "I couldn't forgive myself if either of my children were involved in a preventable accident."

After a moment of silence, Boone asked, "Could you forgive yourself for depriving your children of opportunities to grow?" He wouldn't push too hard, but he couldn't give up, either. "Let him come to the den meeting Wednesday after school. The most strenuous activities they'll do is memorize pledges and make crafts from the handbook. Give him a chance to focus that energy of his on something that interests him. You might even find he'll be less inclined to harass his sister if he has something else to occupy his mind."

At that, Nixie's temper flared. How dare he imply that her son's mischief-making was related to her protectiveness?

"Tell me ... how many children have *you* parented?"

He didn't seem the least put off by her defensiveness, which only disconcerted Nixie even more.

"Not counting the Scouts, none. But not for a lack of wanting."

She peered at him through the darkness. She could tell that, this time, he wasn't teasing.

Somehow this latest revelation didn't rest well with Nixie. It was as though an object she'd always seen as round suddenly turned out to be triangular.

If he'd claimed to be a womanizer or even an Olympic contender, she'd have had no trouble accepting that information. But she'd never seen him as domestic material, perhaps because his competitiveness made him seem like an unsuitable candidate for the give and take of everyday family life.

"What's the matter?" he asked. "Don't you think Boone the Goon would qualify as a family man?"

4

Nixie's eyes jerked up to meet his. "I never thought of you that way. It was a horrible nickname, and I don't know why you used to let people call you that," she said with more vehemence than she'd intended.

He shot her a skeptical glance but said nothing.

Nixie wasn't sure why, but it bothered her to think he doubted her sincerity.

The first drop of rain hit Nixie's cheek and trickled down to her chin. In a few more seconds, she and Boone were running across the soggy field, back to the car.

Doors opened and slammed shut, and bodies dripped water onto the leather upholstery.

Laughing and winded, Nixie said, "We could have walked and gotten no wetter than we are now."

"Ah," Boone corrected with a finger held aloft.

"But then you wouldn't be breathing hard and fogging the windows."

Nixie cut her eyes at him. It was as though time had stood still for fifteen years. Only Ellen was not here to tell her brother to shut up.

"Could we call a truce for the next, say, thirty or forty years?"

Boone put a hand to his chin as if considering her suggestion. "If you want to call a truce, it must mean we're at war and you're losing. If you're losing, that means I get to seize all your property. Personally, I think that sounds like more fun than a truce."

He was not going to do it again. Nixie was not going to let him make her blush or stammer or react in any of those embarrassing ways she did as a kid.

"Look, nobody's going to seize anyone else's property." She tried not to focus on the mental image that accompanied her words. "The only thing I want from you is your promise not to encourage Bethany and Brad in this 'daddy' ad or any future such brainstorms."

He stretched back against the seat and draped his right arm behind her. "I don't want to see them get hurt any more than you do. But," he reminded her, "they did spend their own money for the ad."

"I realize that, but I'm just asking you not to get them overexcited about this cornball idea." In a gesture of annoyance, she swept her hair away from her face and flipped the ends over her shoulder. The damp tendrils fell limply across Boone's arm.

"We're both soaked to the skin. Let's go dry off, and then we'll talk about this some more."

He drove only a block and a half and pulled in at the centuries-old tavern that housed the *Bliss Crier.* Inside, he led her past the empty receptionist's desk and offices that were occupied by desktop publishing systems, large screen dual monitors, and laser printers. In a nod to the past, there was even a large slant-top graphic design desk with a stack of clip art books on top. The modern insides of the building provided a sharp contrast to the historic exterior.

Boone opened a wooden crossbar door and led her up a narrow staircase to a small apartment. With a minimum of furnishings other than bodybuilding equipment and an absence of curtains, it looked like a man's apartment. A Cro-Magnon man's apartment.

Nixie smiled. "How quaint."

"It's not much to look at yet, but it has everything I need." He pointed into the cramped kitchen. "Including a dryer." Without preamble, he peeled off his shirt and tossed it into the machine.

Nixie's eyes were drawn to the broad, firm planes of his chest and abdomen. Liberally covered with golden-brown hair, his torso was so wide she wondered if her arms could encompass it. Which led her to wonder whether it was curiosity or the strange sensation in the pit of her being that made her want to try. The upper part of his arms seemed as big around as her thigh.

Her gaze fell to the purplish mark that began on

his left hip and disappeared beneath the waistband of his trousers. From his casual stance, he appeared not to be aware of the dark bruise or her reaction to it. Yes, indeed, this was a Cro-Magnon's apartment, and here was the resident Cro-Magnon.

"I swear I won't jump your bones. There's even a lock on the bedroom door if you don't trust me."

Nixie jerked her attention away from his hip to the amused expression he wore. "What?"

"I said, give me your dress and I'll throw it in the dryer with my shirt. Come on, I'll get you a robe to wear." He led her down the short hall to his bedroom and rummaged in the drawer for a terry cloth robe, which he tossed to her. Then he retrieved a black T-shirt and pulled it on. Nixie had been relieved to see him covering his bare chest, but the sight of him in that tight shirt was just as distracting.

He left the room and was pulling the door shut when he leaned back in with a grin. "Let me know if you need anything else."

When the door finally clicked shut, Nixie took a big breath to calm her frazzled nerves. "What you *need* is a swift kick for what you're thinking," she muttered to herself. "He didn't ask what you *want*." As a widowed mother of two, she knew she would be wise to forget about those particular wants. At least for now.

Doffing the wet dress, she let it fall to the floor and shrugged on Boone's enormous robe. On him, it was probably knee-length. On her, it fell to the middle of her calves. She wrapped the front flaps tightly about her and knotted the belt around her middle. Even though she still wore her half-slip and camisole, she felt naked underneath the robe.

She was glad, when she emerged from his bedroom, that he made no teasing comments about her appearance. Instead, he took her dress to the kitchen where he started the dryer and returned a moment later with two cups of hot coffee.

Aside from the television and a bench press, the only piece of furniture in the living room was a brown plaid demi-sofa. She sat down and, with a little squeezing, he joined her. Although it was made to seat two people, Nixie was sure it hadn't been designed with Boone in mind.

He had turned at an angle to face her. Having crossed one ankle over the other knee, his thigh hovered disconcertingly over her lap. Trying to ignore his proximity, she attempted once more to elicit his support in discouraging the children from their wild-haired scheme.

"Look, about that ad—"

He looked up and gave her his full attention. It was all Nixie could do to keep from drowning in the ocean-blue depths of his eyes.

"It would make things a lot simpler if any replies were, well, discreetly disposed of." She was acting in the children's best interest, so why did she feel like such a heel for making this simple request?

"This is the kids' ad," Boone said gently. "They're entitled to all the replies that come from it."

Nixie fumed. It was impossible to argue with someone who wielded logic as his weapon. "What about dangerous or crazy people? Surely you know that they're the only kind of people who would answer such an ad."

Boone chuckled. "Does a person have to be dangerous or crazy to look for love or a place in a family?"

"You're ignoring my point," Nixie persisted. "I don't want my kids reading angry or foul letters from someone with an ax to grind."

"You're right."

Nixie breathed a sigh of relief that he was finally beginning to see reason.

"You're their mother," he continued, "and it's certainly within your rights to take away from them whatever you think might be harmful."

The rat! He wasn't giving in after all. He was going to force her into the role of bad guy by making her take away the letters he brought to her children.

Boone set his empty cup on the floor and leaned back, clasping his fingers behind his neck. The thought entered Nixie's head that with this posture, he created a bigger target for a thrown object.

Opting for a more prudent alternative, she followed suit and placed her cup on the floor. She stood. "Obviously, you aren't willing to see reason, so I may as well quit wasting our time."

"Suit yourself," said Boone, making no apology for his inflexibility. "I'll get your dress."

He came back clutching a yellow and black garment that looked as though it would fit a large doll.

"What did you do to my dress? It was almost new!"

Boone at least had the grace to look sheepish. "If I were you, I'd take it back. This sucker shrunk to half its original size."

"Give me that." It was just like Boone Shelton to heap insult on top of injury. It was bad enough having her simple request refused so callously, but now this. She shook out the dress and held it against her. The bottom barely cleared her hips. "There's no way I can wear this home."

Her glare warned him not to make one of his typical smart-alecky replies.

He took the hint, and the ride to Nixie's house was filled with a tense silence. Boone broke the standoff as he pulled into her driveway.

"I'm sorry about your dress. It looks like I owe you a new one."

"You owe me, all right."

She got out before he could come around to open the door. She was furious with him—but not about the dress. That could easily be replaced. Even so, she wanted him to pay ... for the dress, for insisting on giving letters to her children after she'd asked him not to, for implying she wasn't doing a good job of raising her son. Most of all, she wanted him to pay for those years of merciless teasing.

"Yes, sir," she said. "You owe me for a lot more than this dress. You can start paying me back by forgetting that my kids ever placed that crazy ad in your paper."

"I'm sorry." He got out of the car and came around to open her door even though she'd already gotten out, as if either his chivalry or his nearness would soften his answer. "I can't do wrong by your kids just because you asked me to ... even if you are a friend."

"Friend?" How could he have ever considered them such? They'd been at each other's throats all through school, and it looked as though the cycle was starting all over. "If you treat your friends like this, I'm glad I'm not your enemy."

Her voice sounded squeaky, and she hated how she'd let him get to her. With trembling fingers, she untied the terry cloth sash at her waist and yanked off the bulky robe.

"Here," she said, thrusting the garment into his arms. "Don't ever let it be said I accepted any favors from you."

With a haughty whirl, she turned away from him and stormed toward the house. To Boone, in the twilight her white lingerie made her look like a tiny spirit floating across the lawn.

And like a spirit, she was just as hard to pin down. When the apparition disappeared into the house without so much as a glance over her shoulder, Boone got back into his car and drove off.

He wouldn't be able to wear that robe again without thinking of her.

Nixie stomped into the house and slammed the door behind her. Unmindful of her appearance, she huffed into the living room, where her aunt and uncle looked up from their television show.

"Well," said Uncle Jay, "it looks like you had a nice time."

Tarzan eyed her from his cage and let out a jungle yell.

"You—" Not in the mood for the bird's shenanigans, Nixie pointed a finger at the parrot.

"Shut up, stupid!" Tarzan finished for her.

Shhh! If he kept up like that, he was sure to wake the children.

"Nixie, don't argue with the bird." Aunt Lauren got up to cover the cage. "You know he always gets the last word."

With the feathered commentator quieted, Aunt Lauren turned back to Nixie. "Are you all right? Did Boone hurt you?"

Nixie shifted the dress to her other hand and crumpled it. "I'm fine. My dress was ruined in his dryer after we got drenched in a downpour."

Uncle Jay grunted his annoyance. "I lent him my shirt. I don't see why he couldn't have done the same for you."

"He lent me his robe, but I gave it back." At their

questioning glances, she stretched and faked a yawn. "I didn't mean to stay out so late. Thanks for putting the kids to bed."

"Anytime, dear." Aunt Lauren kissed her cheek.

Nixie could tell there were questions her relatives wanted to ask. She was glad they didn't voice them, because she certainly didn't have any answers. As she closed the door behind them, she decided life would be much simpler if she could avoid Boone Shelton altogether.

Over the next week and a half, she tried many times to put him out of her mind but frequently found her thoughts returning to him.

One morning, as she was reading the *Bliss Crier,* she couldn't help noticing the new image the twice-weekly paper sported lately ... more professional and much less biased than when Mr. Yoden had owned the business. Even many of the advertisers who had, over the years, taken their business elsewhere now returned with large, eye-catching displays. One of the new features was an advice column. And, along with the changes in format and content, the name had been changed to the *Bliss Gazette.* She supposed that was Boone's attempt to stop the *Bliss Liar* jokes.

Yes, indeed, he was a man of honor, and the business owners of Bliss knew it. It was just too bad he couldn't—or wouldn't—relax his honor where her kids were concerned. She supposed she should be glad he was so steadfast about doing the right thing, but she wished he could also foresee the problems it could cause.

Regardless of Boone's code of ethics, she couldn't just stand by and watch her kids get hurt—or worse, scared— when they read the letters that might come from their ad.

Nixie had ignored her children's squabbles about who should get the marshmallow stars from the cereal box. Now, however, she looked up to find Brad with his finger poised and ready to flick a piece of cereal at his sister. She gave him a quelling glare, and he reluctantly popped the tidbit into his mouth.

Boone might be the rough-and-tumble type, but her children weren't. They still needed protection, and she was determined to provide it for them. She would just have to be extra diligent with Boone to make sure they were protected from his good intentions.

When Boone showed up unexpectedly the next evening, she didn't let him rattle her composure.

"I didn't know they made Cub Scout uniforms that big," she said, referring to his khaki shirt and pants.

"Mom, he's the den leader," Brad pointed out.

Boone, however, refused to be goaded. "The bigger the kid," he replied, "the bigger the uniform." Turning his attention to Brad, he added, "I'll bet we can get you one in your size, too."

"Can I, Mom?"

She fixed a warning glare on Boone, but he appeared not to notice it. He was certainly the most hardheaded person she'd ever met.

"He missed last week's den meeting," said Boone. "There's plenty of room in my car, so there's no need for him to miss this week, too."

Nixie pushed her hair behind her shoulders with a defiant flip of her wrist. "We've already talked about this."

"We also talked about depriving children of opportunities to grow." To Brad, he said, "What have you achieved in your spare time since I saw you at the play?"

The boy grinned proudly. "I taught Tarzan to bark at Bethany's cat."

Boone opened his hands in a resigned gesture. "I rest my case."

Bethany obviously overheard and came in from another room. "Mom, you've *got* to do something about that kid."

Nixie sighed. She supposed Boone had been telling the truth when he said the most strenuous den meeting activities would be memorizing pledges and making crafts. Maybe she could at least let Brad try it. "He hasn't had supper."

"I'll buy him a burger."

"Friends for life, man!" Brad and Boone exchanged high five. The boy dashed out to the car, then stopped to see what was holding up the den leader.

Boone had been a little slower to leave. Lingering on the porch, he acted as though he wanted to say something else to Nixie. When Brad called out to him, he winked at Nixie and said, "See you in a couple of hours."

His words sounded more like a promise than an idle comment. With a peculiar sense of anticipation, Nixie found herself looking forward to seeing him later that evening.

She watched as Boone and Brad drove away. One large blond man and one small blond boy. To the uninformed, the two could easily pass for father and son.

Less than two hours had gone by when Nixie started worrying. She wasn't used to Brad going away with anyone other than Jay or Lauren. They should have had time to eat a hamburger, attend the hour-long meeting, and return by now. She paced the living room again and pulled the curtain back to peek out. Maybe she shouldn't have let him go after all.

"Chill out, Mom," said Bethany. "He'll be back soon. You ought to enjoy the peace and quiet while you can."

A little more than two hours passed before she heard car doors slam, followed by excited male voices.

Brad entered, carrying a large department store bag. Boone smiled in a self-satisfied way. It was enough to make Nixie wonder what mischief they'd been up to.

Boone nudged the boy. "Show her what you got."

That was all the prompting Brad needed. In seconds, the floor was scattered with official Cub Scout uniform parts, including cap, neckerchief, and patches.

"Where did you get all this?" Nixie asked, puzzled by the unexpected purchase.

Boone cleared his throat. "After the meeting, I figured we weren't too far from the mall, so we saved you a trip."

The mall was very much out of their way, but before Nixie could point this out, Brad declared, "I'm a real Scout now, Mom. Next time, I won't be the only one wearing play clothes."

"Who said anything about next time? I thought you were just going to try it out and see if you liked it." Turning to Boone with one hand on her hip, she waited for an explanation.

"He did try it out, and he liked it. Since we got the uniform tonight, you'll have time to sew the patches on before the next meeting."

He seemed quite pleased with his forethought,

but Nixie wished he hadn't taken it upon himself to do this. She felt pushed into a corner.

"You really shouldn't have done it," she said, sweeping a hand to indicate the items Brad was admiring, piece by piece.

Boone sat on the couch. "It was the least I could do after what happened to your dress. I would have bought you a replacement, but I don't know your size."

"Don't worry about it. In my job, I don't wear anything fancier than jeans and T-shirts."

Brad interrupted by jostling Boone's knee. "Don't forget to give this to Bethany."

Boone took the small white box from the boy and handed it to Bethany. "We saw this in the store and thought of you."

Nixie watched as her daughter tentatively opened the box and lifted out a pair of miniature satin ballet slippers on a pink velvet rope. "Thank you," she whispered. Gingerly, she draped the necklace over her head. "This is beautiful. Whose idea was it?"

As one, Brad and Boone pointed at each other.

"I'm going to go look at it in the mirror," she said and ran upstairs.

"I'm going to try on my new uniform." Brad disappeared up the stairs behind his sister.

In those few seconds, the room fell silent. Even the parrot was quiet for a change.

Nixie settled into the chair beside Boone and

tucked her feet under her. "Don't you know Santa's not supposed to return for another nine months?"

"I like your kids. They're good people."

Nixie looked at him suspiciously. She thought he had been joking, but one look at the sincere smile on his handsome face told her he meant what he said. Hadn't he seen by now what little stinkers her children could be?

The few other men who'd come to her home had chosen not to return after the first visit. She had suspected they'd been put off by the mere presence of the children, yet Boone was a man who claimed to like them even though they could be very rambunctious at times.

She turned her attention to him. "How's your forehead?"

Boone lifted a hand and touched the spot above his eye. Nixie admired the way his simple motion caused the muscles to bunch in his upper arm.

"Back to normal."

Slipping back into the role she'd played so many years ago, she shot back, "I knew that hard head of yours would come in handy someday."

Boone was just as quick with his reply. "It's even harder now. I don't take no for an answer." He leaned forward, bracing his elbows on his knees. "I still feel bad about shrinking your dress. Let me take you to dinner Friday night."

"That's not necessary. Besides, you've more than made up for it by buying Brad's uniform."

"I would have done that anyway." He leaned back again and pushed away the shaggy blond hair that had fallen over his eyebrow. When Nixie started to make excuses, he repeated, "I don't take no for an answer."

She studied the man who had once been her chief tormentor. Why was he being so nice now? This side of Boone Shelton unsettled her. She was used to dealing with his orneriness and teasing, aggravating as it was. But when he was being nice like this, she couldn't help suspecting he was up to something.

She shook off the feeling of unease. Maybe he was truly repentant for what he'd done to her dress and was honestly trying to make it up to her. If that was the case, perhaps she should let him assuage his guilt and be done with it.

"What if we say it's just for old times' sake?" he prompted.

Maybe if she said yes, he'd satisfy his guilt, she'd satisfy her belief that they could never get along, and then they'd both go their separate ways. "I get off at five," she said, "unless I happen to be tending a hit-and-run victim."

"That should be no problem since one of the Cub Scouts wrote down the license number of the car that hit me. The driver is to appear in court next month." He laughed. "Funny thing is, we had just talked at the meeting before that about what to do if you witness a crime. Those kids remember more than you'd think."

There was no mistaking the pride in his voice when he talked about the young Scouts. A chill came over her as she realized that was the same tone Paul had used when bragging about Bethany and Brad.

At times such as this, Boone Shelton actually seemed tender and sensitive, an image that did not go with his boisterous, rough nature. It looked like she was going to have to rethink her impressions of him.

5

Dinner Friday night was another occasion in which Nixie was forced to look at her childhood nemesis in a different light.

She'd been expecting him to take her to the Rib Rack, a popular local restaurant that featured lots of beef and a casual—even rowdy—atmosphere. Instead, he'd surprised her by making reservations at Jean Jacques in a nearby town.

He'd surprised her further by recommending an excellent chicken dish to Nixie and ordering their meals in fluent French. This was certainly not the monosyllabic boy she remembered from high school.

While they waited for their dinner, Boone asked her a few questions, and soon she was telling him all about Paul. Not just the good things that people tend to remember after a loved one is gone, but she even told him that her husband had been a workaholic, something she'd never shared with anyone else.

When she explained how they'd been on their way to a weekend getaway at a mountain cabin to escape the stress of his job and of tending to the two babies, she appreciated Boone's quiet understanding.

And when she described how she had tried helplessly to free her unconscious husband after she'd regained consciousness herself, from the flaming car after he'd fallen asleep at the wheel and crashed into a tree, she was thankful for Boone's non-pitying empathy.

It wasn't until their desserts arrived that she realized she had monopolized the entire conversation. "I'm sorry," she said. "I didn't mean to bore you."

Boone looked across the table at the exciting woman sitting opposite him. "You don't bore me." He wanted to add, "You fascinate me," but thought better of it. With his record of teasing, he knew she wouldn't take him seriously.

"Well, enough about me," she said, plunging her spoon into the strawberry parfait. "Tell me about your newspaper. You seem to be making quite a few improvements."

"There's not much to tell," he admitted. "I saw my hometown newspaper on the brink of going under, so I bought it and am trying to turn it around."

"I've been enjoying the new advice column, 'Ask Aunt Alice.' Is she a local person?"

Boone tensed. He bought a few seconds by mashing the remaining crumbs of his seven-layer cake onto his fork. "Alice is a very private person," he said at last. "She feels more comfortable staying in the background."

Nixie nodded her agreement. "I suppose it would get tiresome to have people telling her their problems every time she goes to the store or to get her hair done."

He smiled. "Yes, I suppose it's something like that."

Nixie dabbed the napkin to her mouth and flashed him a decidedly sneaky smile. "Do you always reserve the front page for catastrophic, earth-shaking news?"

Boone paused a moment before answering. From that smug smile to her intense interest in his plans for the newspaper, it was clear she was baiting him. Always open for a little sport, he bit.

"Only the most incredible news goes on page one."

"Like the opossum that gave birth in Mrs. Masten's garbage can?"

"It's not every day a person finds baby wildlife in her garbage can."

"If the rescue squad were to sponsor a fundraiser, would you put that on page one?"

Boone smiled his amusement. The woman was definitely persistent. "It depends on whether the photo opportunity rates right up there with Mrs. Masten's possums."

"Just what I wanted to hear. I'm sure you'll want to assign a reporter to cover our project, as soon as I figure out what it's going to be. I'll let you know the date as soon as the committee decides."

"Tell me, why is it so important for the rescue squad to receive news coverage in the *Gazette?*"

"It's the fire department, too, actually. We're having membership drives, and public awareness makes people more willing to donate money to buy more modern equipment and convert to an upgraded 911 system."

"What's wrong with the current system?"

"Right now, it won't accept text messages. The system can only take voice calls."

It seemed fairly obvious, but as a journalist he had to ask, "Why can't people just call? Seems like it would be easier and quicker to give the information that way?"

A shadow fell over Nixie's delicate features. He knew from experience that she wasn't as delicate as she looked, but right now she seemed almost ... fragile.

"The first person who stopped to help Paul and me was deaf. His text wouldn't go through. I was unconscious, so he had to wait for the next passerby to stop before they could give instructions to the dispatcher." Nixie grew silent for a moment before continuing. "Paul might have been saved if the fire department had arrived a few minutes sooner."

Boone frowned and idly rubbed where the hair tickled the nape of his neck. She was blaming herself for her husband's death. No wonder she was so insistent in her efforts to publicize the rescue department's activities.

He reached into his pocket and pulled out a pair of dark-rimmed glasses, then withdrew his ever-present pad and pen from his coat pocket. "This sounds like a story." Jotting down the essentials, he said, "I'll have the feature writer contact you next week."

Nixie was shaking her head. "I don't want a story about me. I'd be happier if you'd send your reporter to cover the squad's publicity project ... when we pick a date for it, that is."

He figured now would be the time to tell her about the Cub Scout event next month. "All right," he said, tucking the pad and pen back in his coat pocket, "but I'd suggest you make it any day but the twenty-fifth. That's the weekend of the family camporee."

Nixie looked at him blankly. It didn't sound like something that should concern her.

"The Cub Scout camp-out," Boone clarified. "Brad is expected to come. And you and Bethany should be there that morning and afternoon for Family Day."

Nixie didn't like the idea of this. What had started as a few den meetings where her son would memorize pledges and make crafts had now ballooned into the kind of activity she feared for him to be involved in. Why, he could become lost in the woods, get bitten by a snake, or any number of other things she'd rather not think about.

Boone must have misread her concern for reluctance to participate. "You won't have to stay for the whole thing," he assured. "That night is for Scouts and fathers only."

Nixie didn't have time to respond before he caught his error and suggested, "Perhaps Mr. Cordaire would like to fill in this time."

The panic she'd felt a moment ago was now replaced by amusement at his suggestion. "Uncle Jay sleeping in a tent? He might go for it if you could promise him a portable TV that would pick up HBO." She shook her head. "Besides, his snoring would keep everyone else awake."

Elbows resting on the table and fingers steepled, Boone was quiet for a moment. In that suit and those glasses, he looked almost ... studious. Quite a different picture from the time he'd appeared at her door in shredded jeans and a shirt with the sleeves hacked off.

"Then, unless you or Brad object, I'd like for him to be with me that night."

On the surface, it sounded like a sweet offer, but Nixie couldn't allow it if he was doing it out of pity. Worse, what if Brad mistakenly read something into the situation?

What if he became dependent on Boone as a

father figure of sorts? She couldn't allow her son to be hurt. In the short time he'd known Boone, Brad already seemed to idolize him.

"I don't think that's a good idea."

From the way he clenched his jaw and narrowed his eyes, Nixie knew her comment had been carelessly blunt. She hadn't meant to hurt him, but she couldn't allow her child to be hurt, either.

"Fine, but if you can't find someone else, my offer still stands. Brad's a Cub Scout now, Nixie, and I expect him to be there and participate fully, come hell or high water ... or rescue squad publicity event."

His meaning was clear. He was warning her not to plan her media event for that day and use it as an excuse not to attend the camporee. But he should know by now that he could no longer tease, cajole, or even threaten her into bending to his will.

Boone Shelton had always managed to pop into her life at the most inconvenient times—such as the time he ruined her date with Craig Curtis, the high school hunk—and he never failed to create turmoil with her well-laid plans.

Well, this time he wouldn't do it. She wouldn't let him. Although Nixie was happy that Brad had found a friend in Boone and that the Scout leader encouraged him to act more responsibly, she was leery of Boone's intrusion into their lives. After all, he was encouraging her son to participate in new and risky activities. Her worst fear was that something terrible might happen to one of her children.

Tonight was Friday, and Boone wasn't expected to come to the house until next Wednesday, when he picked up Brad for the weekly den meeting. Maybe by then she'd come up with a way to discourage her son—her baby—from going on the camporee. He was so small and vulnerable, and he needed to be protected from Boone's good intentions.

Boone stood and walked around to her chair. He offered her a hand up to escort her from the restaurant and flashed a warm smile that threatened to melt her resolve.

A frightening thought flitted through her mind. Who would protect *her* from Boone and his good intentions?

The next morning Nixie was still wondering at her reaction to Boone when he'd stood on her front porch and said good night. For what must have been one of the most insane moments of her life, she'd found herself wishing he would kiss her.

Instead, Uncle Jay had switched on the porch light and peeked out through one of the three small windowpanes in the door. Even if Boone had been inclined to kiss her, Nixie was certain that the sight of her grinning uncle would have been enough to squelch the notion.

She hadn't slept well and chose to blame her restlessness on the rich food she'd eaten at dinner. When she awoke early to the sound of water gurgling down the rainspout and thunder clapping in the distance, she got up and pitched her fitful energy into Saturday morning chores.

Brad dragged a broom from the utility room and started pushing it ineffectually around the dining room.

As Bethany passed him with a dust rag in her hand, Nixie heard her grumble, "Do you think Mom was a drill sergeant in a former life?"

Brad nodded his agreement.

She had been working them hard this morning. But, as her parents had taught her and her brother, a little hard work never hurt anyone. Besides, once they were finished, they'd have the rest of the day to play. Nixie opened the dishwasher and started putting the clean dishes away. With a little smile, she ordered, "No talking in the ranks."

They obediently went about their work. A few minutes later, Bethany came rushing into the kitchen. "Mom, there's a man in the bushes out front!"

Nixie put the last cup in the cabinet. "Honey, it's pouring outside. I don't think—" One look at her daughter's panicked face assured her that Bethany had seen *something*. "It's probably just a neighbor's dog," she said. "Show me where you saw it."

Bethany pulled back the curtain. See? He's down on all fours, and his shoes are sticking out from under the bush."

"Want me to get the gun?" Brad shouted.

"We don't have a gun. Go get your baseball bat."

The figure slowly backed out from under the bush. When he rose, Nixie could see that he was tall, even though he stood hunched against the rain. Through the downpour, it looked as though he were hiding something under his jacket. He turned and started toward the house.

By now Bethany was in a panic. "I'm going to call Uncle Jay. He'll know what to do."

Brad returned with the baseball bat. "I'm going to go out the back door, sneak up on him, and bash him over the head!" He swung the bat for emphasis and almost knocked over a lamp.

"No!" Nixie took the bat from her son. "Go make sure the door is locked. Bethany, get off the phone in case we need to call the police."

"Uncle Jay's not home! What if that man tries to kill us?"

"Bethany, get a grip," Nixie urged. "Try to set a good example for Brad."

Brad, by now, was unlocking the front door. He pulled it open and rushed out into the rain toward the stranger.

"Brad!" Nixie raced after him, the bat clutched tightly in her hand.

Just as her son reached him, the man looked up, his smiling blue eyes shining through the rain.

"Kind of wet for a ball game, don't you think?"

Nixie's emotions warred between relief and indignation. "Boone, you almost scared the life out of us! What are you doing skulking around in my yard?"

"Getting wet." He opened one side of his jacket and enveloped Brad in the way a hen would protect a chick with her wing. "Why don't we talk inside where it's more comfortable?"

Once inside, there was no opportunity for her to lay into him as she'd intended. There were towels to fetch and muddy shoes to contend with. And just when she was about to give Boone a piece of her mind, he removed a soggy bundle of brown fluff from inside his jacket and placed it on the floor.

The animal was so soiled and matted she could hardly tell what it was until it meowed. "Oh, my," said Nixie. "It's that stray cat that's been hanging around here for the past week. We tried to catch it, but it was always too quick for us."

Boone took a dry towel and wrapped it around the squirming kitten. "I saw it limping toward the bush when I drove up."

"Mom, its leg is hurt," said Bethany. "Look, it's bleeding."

Nixie sighed and got up to retrieve the first aid kit. "Don't get too attached to it," she told the kids. "We don't have room for another animal."

At their groans, Nixie realized the kitten would be easier to remove from their lives than the two-legged animal that had brought it in.

A short while later, its brown fur dried and the

minor wound on its leg tended, the kitten slept in a cardboard box lined with an old blanket.

Nixie looked over at the big man who dominated her couch. Though he was older now and small lines marked the corners of his eyes, he was still protecting those smaller than himself.

Boone watched with interest as she repacked the antibiotic cream in the carrying case and snapped the lid shut. "Why do you keep clean underwear in your first aid kit?"

Nixie smiled at the reminder of her son's goofy sense of humor. "Brad put them there in case he gets hurt and has to go to the hospital."

Boone turned to Brad and nudged the boy with his elbow. "Did you get tired of your mom's lectures?"

Brad gave his new pal a beleaguered look that said more clearly than words, "Women!"

Although she was the subject of their shared joke, Nixie was glad to see that her mischievous son admired such a solid, stable role model as Boone. Even though Boone was somewhat pushy about urging her to let Brad become more involved in Scouting, it was clear that his intentions were good and that he could be a positive influence on a boy.

Remembering their conversation of last night, she wondered if he had come to pressure her into letting Brad go on the camporee. Due to her lack of sleep last night, she doubted her sluggish mind could quickly come up with a reasonable excuse to keep the boy home, where he'd be safe.

"Your ears must be bionic if you heard that cat's distress call all the way from your apartment," Nixie told him.

"Actually," he said, brandishing two envelopes, "I came to deliver these. Forgot to give them to Bethany and Brad yesterday," he added.

"Letters?" Bethany stopped rubbing the kitten and stepped closer to Boone.

"Somebody answered our ad!" Brad crowed.

Nixie shot Boone a look that should have withered his socks, but he just grinned back at her.

She had to give him credit, though. Before he let them open the envelopes, he talked about how they shouldn't get their hopes up if someone sounded good in a letter, and they shouldn't be discouraged if the respondents weren't suitable.

"There are all kinds of people out there," he told them. "And you take a risk when you ask them to correspond with you."

"I'm going in the other room," Nixie announced. "I want nothing to do with this." Nevertheless, she found herself loitering near the archway leading into the living room where she could hear all that was said.

"She'll come around," Brad said. "All we gotta do is find her a good one."

Boone moved over so there was room for a child to sit on either side of him. Out of the corner of his eye, he could see Nixie making a pretense of wiping fingerprints off the wall.

"Okay," he told the kids, "let's see what this one says." He unfolded the letter, and they read it together.

I don't write good but if you wud call me I wil tell you all abot myself.

A phone number was included under the sloppily scrawled signature.

"What do you think?" he asked them.

Bethany was quick to offer her opinion. "No."

Brad shrugged. "He can't spell, but maybe he's a nice person."

"He's not the one for us." Bethany was insistent. "How could he help us with our homework? And I don't think Mom would go for him because she'd want someone who reads a lot. People who read usually spell better than people who don't read."

"Good point," said Boone. He balled up the letter.

"What about the other one?" Brad asked.

"This one sounds better," Boone told them. He unfolded the letter and read it aloud so Nixie could hear.

I was interested in your advertisement because I'm very lonely and want to share in the love of a close family relationship. Realizing that no one is perfect, I would accept you just as you are. I ask only that you afford me the same courtesy. I believe family members should talk to each other every day, and I look forward to planning some wonderful family activities with you. Please write soon. If you don't, I'll be patient. I have plenty of time.

Brad grabbed the letter. "Hey, he sounds pretty good."

Boone noticed that Nixie had stopped what she was doing to listen.

Bethany was looking at the return address on the envelope. "What does 1988476 mean?"

Boone studied the envelope a moment. "That's his prison number."

"Boone, may I speak with you in here?" Nixie thrummed her fingers on the wall she'd just wiped down.

When he came into the dining room, Nixie had to tilt her head back to look up at him. That didn't keep her from shaking a finger at him as if he were one of her own children. "That's exactly why I didn't want them to go through with this foolishness!"

"Don't worry, Nix." Boone clasped her hand and curled her index finger down with the rest. "Your kids are smart enough not to get you hooked up with a felon."

"How do you know he's a felon?"

"Return address," he replied. "He's in the maximum security unit."

"Oh, good grief!"

Quietly, so that only she could hear, he leaned closer and murmured in her ear, "Wouldn't it be simpler to forget about finding a stranger to fill the position and start looking at candidates you know?"

Nixie almost stopped breathing. Was he recommending himself? Or was it just wishful thinking on her part? She had to get a grip on herself. Maybe Aunt Lauren was right ... maybe she'd been too long without a man in her life. Maybe, too, she was subconsciously trying to fill that void with someone safe and familiar.

He was certainly familiar, but Nixie doubted she was safe around him. For all she knew, his comment could have been another teasing joke. Well, she'd play along.

"Yes, you're probably right," she admitted. "Let's see, there's old Mr. Finch who cleans our offices every week. Why, did you know he's expecting his four-teenth grandchild next month? Such a dear man. And so lonely since his Clara passed away."

She casually rubbed another fingerprint from the wall. He was playing hardball, refusing to grant her even a glimmer of a smile as he pretended to believe her.

"Then there's always Markey Evans down the block," she continued. "He's only sixteen, but I hear he has incredible buns."

"Mom!" cried Bethany. "You don't have to go and tell everyone what I said."

Precious, who had earlier run terrorized from the room when Brad had pretended to "sweep" her with the broom, now returned and noticed the little brown furball trying to climb out of its box. Though normally timid, the older cat crept closer to the box, hissed loudly, and took a swat at the tiny intruder.

All four humans leaped to the kitten's defense,

and Precious was quickly banished to the utility room. Bethany was visibly shaken by her pet's uncharacteristic display of hostility.

"Precious is usually so sweet. Why would she try to hurt that innocent little kitten?"

Nixie put an arm around her daughter. "I'm sure she wasn't trying to hurt the kitten. She was just trying to protect her domain."

"Her domain?"

"Yes. Her turf. Precious considers this house her own. And when a new animal comes in, it feels like that animal is invading her territory."

"It's my fault," said Boone. "I shouldn't have brought it in here. I'll take it to the pound when I leave. Since it's so young, maybe someone will adopt it."

"And maybe they won't," Bethany declared.

Brad grabbed Boone's arm. "Why don't you take it home with you?"

Nixie tried to imagine the kitten living in that stark bachelor apartment. It would be alone all day while Boone worked. And Boone probably worked overtime occasionally, not to mention the time that he spent with the Scouts.

Boone slowly shook his head. "Sorry, pal. It just wouldn't work out."

Pushing aside her earlier comment about not having enough room for another animal, Nixie impulsively blurted out, "It's going to need medical atten-

LORI WILDE & & CAROLYN GREENE

tion until that leg heals. We may as well let it stay here so I can keep an eye on it."

The kids exploded with cheers, and Boone shot her his familiar teasing grin. "You always were a soft touch," he said.

He was grinning, but the way he said it made her think about soft touches ... *his* soft touches on her heated body. If she weren't careful, he'd have her blushing like the shy teenager she used to be.

"I guess I'll let y'all get back to your housework," he said, heading for the door. His hand on the knob, he stopped and turned to Brad. "I expect to see you at the family camporee next weekend."

For the next week, Brad could talk of nothing else. Nixie had reluctantly agreed to let him go, but she frequently quizzed him with what-if scenarios to prepare him for an emergency. By the end of the week, she'd taught him what to do in case he got bitten by a snake, lost in the woods, cut, or otherwise injured. Still not satisfied, she came up with several uncommon scenarios so he'd be prepared for those, too.

At Nixie's urging, Brad asked Jay to accompany him on the campout, but the older man declined, saying his bad back needed the comfort of his bed at home.

She thought of asking her younger brother to spend the weekend with Brad, but Ryan's wife was due to deliver their first child at any time.

Brad settled the issue after returning home from

his weekly den meeting. Nixie smiled at her son in his navy-blue uniform. He was so proud of being a Scout, he'd started wearing it to school on the day of the meeting, claiming he didn't have enough time to change after school. He wouldn't even hold Tarzan on meeting days for fear the bird might damage or soil the shirt.

"Mom, guess what?" he said and slammed his Scout manual down on the kitchen table before raiding the cookie jar. "I asked Boone to be my dad for the weekend when we go camping."

Nixie stiffened. This was just what she had feared would happen. Brad had often said he wished he had a father like other kids did. He'd even pretended sometimes that Jay was his father.

What if her son transferred his need for a strong male figure to Boone? He had moved away from Bliss once. He could do it again.

"What did Boone say?" Nixie prompted, praying he'd had the foresight not to build up the boy's hopes.

Brad shrugged and munched his cookie. "He said no one could take the place of my real dad, but that he would be my mentor—whatever that is."

Nixie's heart lodged in her throat. Boone hadn't changed a bit. After he'd antagonized her until she thought she could stand it no more, he would do something endearing like this. She supposed that was the only reason they'd managed to maintain a semblance of friendship during their school years.

"Can I take Tarzan with me on the camping trip?"

"Absolutely not."

One out-of-control family member on the trip was more than enough. Even so, she grinned at the image of all the trouble both Brad and Tarzan could scheme up for Boone.

❧ 6 ❧

By the time Saturday came, Bethany was dead set against going. "I don't see why I have to go to Brad's dumb Scout camp."

Nixie gave her daughter a look that warned her not to start an argument in front of company.

Boone picked up Brad's sleeping bag to take it to his car. "Look on the bright side," he told her. "You might meet some cute older Scouts." He tugged her ponytail and went out the door, Brad close on his heels.

Nixie reached into the refrigerator for the last juice box that had been pushed to the back, then dumped ice into the cooler. "We're just going to be there for the day. It's a family thing."

"Well, I don't see why we couldn't ask Uncle Jay and Aunt Lauren to come," she retorted.

"Uncle Jay and Aunt Lauren are in town shopping

for a new living room set. Now, stop arguing and be a good sport."

Nixie and Bethany carried the cooler to the front door, and Nixie noticed that Boone and Brad had returned and were standing in front of the bird cage.

"Nice bird," Boone said as Nixie approached. He turned to the green-and-red feathered chatterbox and said, "I've heard your Tarzan yodel and your giggle. Not to mention some rude comments. Say something else," he urged.

The bird tilted his head and stared mutely at him.

"Come on, I know you can do it. Can you talk?"

The children looked at each other. Nixie could tell they were thrilled Boone had set himself up for the smart-alecky reply that was sure to come. Brad had taught it to the bird for just such an occasion. She smiled as she anticipated Boone's surprise.

Tarzan cocked his head and peered up at Boone. "I can talk," the bird quipped in its croaky voice. "Can you fly?"

The children burst into hysterical laughter. Boone stepped back from the cage and stared openmouthed at the green joker. The wing flapping and the long-winded laugh that Tarzan graced him with made it seem as if he, too, were amused.

"What's the matter?" Nixie goaded. "Haven't you ever had a conversation with a bird before?" She loved dishing out the teasing for a change.

Boone caught her eye, and it was clear he planned to get even. No matter. The shocked expression on his face was worth whatever mischievous deed he had planned for her.

His face a mask of pure innocence, Boone turned to Brad and asked, "How long does it take him to learn something new?"

"About a week or two," Brad said proudly. "Sometimes quicker if he thinks what you're teaching him sounds interesting."

Nixie reminded them of the time, and each picked up something to carry to the car. All but Boone. He was still standing in front of the cage, muttering something to the bird. When he caught Nixie watching him, he joined the rest of them in the foyer and picked up the cooler. "I was just telling him goodbye."

"Have a birdiful day!" Tarzan sang out.

Boone gave her a puzzled glance. "How does he do that?"

"Do what?"

"Know when to say things."

Pleased to have witnessed his being caught off guard for the second time that morning, Nixie just smiled and said, "Sometimes I think he's the smartest one in the family."

The camporee was being held at a nearby state park. Nixie and Bethany set up the picnic while Boone and the other Scout leaders taught the young charges how to erect their tents. As they waited for the boys to finish, she and Bethany explored the area.

Nixie was glad to see the park wasn't as "uncivilized" as she'd anticipated. The picnic tables where they would have lunch were protected by a shelter, and although it was too cool for swimming, the small man-made lake would provide good fishing for the Scouts. A nearby bathhouse offered running water. A clearing in the woods sported rough, split-log benches placed in a semicircle around a large backdrop of plyboard painted white. Here the boys could gather for movies tonight and for chapel in the morning. Nixie was also pleased to note that the ranger's shack was less than a mile away. She'd have to remember to tell Brad that, in case of an emergency and he was unable to get a cell signal, he could call her from there.

After the Scouts came back from setting up their tents and ate lunch, there wasn't time for anyone to get bored. Boone's den and interested family members went horseback riding while others separated to go fishing or hiking. An avid horse lover, Bethany ceased griping for the duration of the trail ride.

On their return to the barn, one of Nixie's fears came true. Alonzo, a boy whose father had not been able to attend and who would also be sharing a tent with Boone, got stung by a horsefly. While Nixie examined the red, swollen area on the boy's wrist, Brad ran to get his knapsack.

"I'll take care of it," Brad announced. He seemed eager to prove that he was able to handle this minor crisis, just as he and Nixie had rehearsed at home.

Nixie stepped back and watched as her son retrieved a small tube containing a greenish solution and dabbed the sponge tip to Alonzo's skin.

Boone sidled up to her. "You should be proud of Brad. He's good Scout material." He absentmindedly rubbed his arm, and Nixie noted the strength in it. "He's a mechanical whiz, too. He put that tent up before I finished explaining how to do it."

His compliment warmed her, probably more than if it had come from someone else. She was, indeed, proud of her son ... and he didn't have to erect a pup tent or tend a bee sting to inspire that feeling. He was a great kid purely on his own merits. She still didn't feel comfortable leaving him this weekend, and Alonzo's run-in with the horsefly made her even more nervous.

"Looks like Alonzo was bee bait," she said a bit more harshly than she intended. "I just hope Brad won't be bear bait."

Boone put an arm around her shoulders. If not for her reaction to it, it might have seemed like a brotherly gesture. That, and the tender look he cast her way, made her feel safe and secure, as if his strong arms could protect her from any danger.

"Brad's a smart kid who can watch out for himself," he said. "And even if he doesn't, I will."

His assurance helped some but not enough.

"I forgot to tell him what to do if he comes across a rabid raccoon."

Boone squeezed her shoulder. "Don't worry."

"That's easy for you to say," she muttered.

"Tell you what," he said. "How do you feel about giving a short first aid lesson to the boys? You could help some of them earn a badge," he urged.

Nixie knew he was trying to divert her attention away from the potential dangers that existed for her son. She let him. It was too frustrating to keep imagining the worst.

After the impromptu first aid class, she left her son, knowing he would be safe with Boone ... even if her heart was not.

The Scouts had settled down around the campfire to toast their marshmallows, and one of the boys started the age-old tradition of telling scary stories. It wasn't long before little Alonzo was frightened out of his wits. To Boone's gratitude, Brad distracted his friend by telling funny anecdotes about his Uncle Jay's pranks. Jay's antics were funny, but the kid's story-telling ability was even funnier. Before long, Alonzo's fears were quieted, and he was trying to top the others with his own wacky tales.

Boone's eyes were drawn back to Brad. In the flickering firelight, the boy's small features and infectious smile reminded him of Nixie. Unlike his mother, however, Brad had a dimple in his right cheek and wispy blond hair. A small, vertical scar from an earlier mishap was evident on the left side of his chin. The boy was sure to be a ladies' man in a few years. Boone only hoped Brad wouldn't be as shy and awkward around girls as Boone had been around Nixie.

Boone hadn't had the benefit of his own father's experience and advice because his parents had divorced shortly before his mother brought them to Bliss to live. His father hadn't visited or even kept up support payments. Boone had to hand it to his mother for never once calling the guy a bum. Which he was.

And now Brad didn't have benefit of a father's advice. Boone chuckled as he recalled the day the two youngsters had come into his office and informed him they wanted to place an ad for a daddy.

If it had been his choice, he would have been their daddy from the start. He'd planned to graduate from college, get his career established, and go back to Bliss to pursue Nixie in earnest. But, as he'd prepared to enter his third year of college, his sister had written in one of her regular letters that the girl who'd stolen his heart had already married someone else.

He couldn't blame Nixie. He'd teased her so ruthlessly she'd probably been glad to see him go.

He'd been so distraught, he went to a college

hangout, met Cheryl, and proposed within six months. The marriage had lasted less than two years.

Maybe if he didn't screw things up this time, he could have another chance with Nixie. He smiled. Maybe, someday, he'd offer fatherly advice to the kid at his elbow and spare him the same grief he'd known.

He playfully grabbed Brad by the back of the neck, gave a light squeeze, and whispered in his ear, "Better get in the tent before the vampire bats come out."

Unfazed, the boy rolled his eyes at the imaginary threat but did as he was asked.

Later, after they'd settled into their sleeping bags, Brad and Alonzo started telling him about school, their pets, and the latest stock car race Brad had watched on television. Boone made a mental note to take the Scouts to the races on one of their future outings.

"What was that noise?" Alonzo whispered.

Boone listened. At first, all he could hear was crickets chirping and the murmuring from fathers and sons in nearby tents. Then he heard the distinctive sound of dried leaves and twigs crackling.

"Maybe it's a raccoon," Brad suggested.

It was bigger than a raccoon, Boone was certain, but he didn't want to scare the boys. "Maybe." He got up and opened the tent flap. "I'm going to take a look."

He'd forgotten the flashlight, but the moon was

full so he could make out the dim shadows of rounded pup tents and nearby trees.

Leaves rustled again, and he turned to the source of the noise. The shape lurking behind a tree was definitely not animal. Boone's first thought was that one of the campers had answered nature's call, but the figure seemed too small for a father and too large for a Scout.

He moved closer, wishing he'd thought to bring his knife. For all he knew, it could be someone trying to harm the unwary campers. When he realized he couldn't get any closer without the intruder hearing or spotting him, he made a tackle that would have been the envy of any semi-pro football player.

The high-pitched scream that followed nearly deafened him.

7

"Boone, what is it?" Brad called out. "Are you all right?"

At first Boone thought he imagined the soft curves beneath him, but when he caught scent of the floral perfume that was her trademark, Boone knew it could be no one other than Nixie.

Flashlight beams danced around them as a couple of fathers came to see what all the commotion was about.

"It's okay," Boone told them. "It's just a hiker who got lost. Everything's under control."

He only wished everything *was* under control. His body was betraying him badly, and Nixie's squirming was making it worse.

Thankfully, the men went back to their respective tents, and Brad had apparently accepted his explanation of what was happening. Boone turned his attention back to Nixie. He didn't move off of her but just raised up on his hands and hovered over her.

"Don't you think it's late for a hike?"

The sound that came out of her was close to a growl. Boone couldn't help thinking he'd like to try to elicit a moan. But Nixie quickly let him know he could forget that notion.

"Are you going to get off of me, or do I have to use what I learned in self-defense class?"

Boone laughed. From her position, she could do little more than wiggle and squirm, and those were *not* good self-defense measures. He got up and helped her to her feet. He let his hand linger at her waist and was pleased when she didn't step away.

"Let me guess," he persisted. "You were thinking about the daddy candidates and decided to come ask me to apply for the position."

She lowered her head. "Boone, quit teasing. I already feel silly enough as it is for getting caught lurking in the bushes."

With the back of his knuckle, he gently stroked her chin until she looked up at him. "What makes you think I'm teasing?"

She grew silent for a long moment, long enough for Boone to think she might take him up on his offer to apply for the job of daddy to her children. For a brief instant, he dared to hope.

"I—I was worried about Brad," she said softly. "I wanted to make sure he's all right."

His hopes dashed, Boone let out his breath in a puff of disappointment.

Apparently reading the sound as a snort of disgust, Nixie stepped out of his grasp and turned away from him.

"I figured you wouldn't understand. But that's okay. I'm used to your kind of attitude." She stepped past him and moved toward the tent. "I'll just take a peek at Brad, tell him good night, and leave."

Boone reached out for her, his fingers closing around her tiny wrist. "No."

Nixie hesitated, then tried to pull her arm away from him. When he didn't relax his grip, she must have realized the futility of struggling with him and stood still. Even in the darkness, Boone could see her straighten her shoulders the way she used to do whenever she was on the losing end of an argument.

"No?"

He lowered his voice. "You show your face in that camp tonight, and your son won't be able to show his face in school next week." Still gripping her wrist, he pulled her to him and gently patted her arm. "I know you don't want to make him the laughingstock of all his friends, but that's exactly what would happen if anyone finds out you were here tonight."

She turned and looked toward the camp, needing to be assured that her little boy was safe and happy.

"Come on," he said. "I'll walk you to your car."

Someone unzipped the tent flap and stepped outside. "Whatcha doing, Boone?"

Nixie instinctively made a step toward her son, then stopped.

Boone motioned for Nixie to stay where she was while he went to the tent to retrieve his forgotten flashlight. "Go back inside and stay there," he told Brad. "I'm going to take the hiker back to the parking area."

The boy went back into the tent as directed and let out a big laugh. "Hey, Alonzo, can you believe some dork is out hiking at this time of night!"

Boone smiled as he rezipped the tent flap. With the flashlight beam to illuminate their path, he started walking with Nixie at his side. After that comment, he doubted Nixie would ever let on that she'd been here tonight.

"He's going to be all right, you know."

She walked beside him in silence.

"Where's Bethany?" he asked.

Nixie took his hand as they stepped over a root. "She's spending the night at my aunt and uncle's." They walked a little farther before they reached the asphalt. "My car is parked over there, near yours."

He held his hand out for her keys and unlocked the vehicle for her. It was small, like its owner, the lines sleek and slightly rounded. He wondered if she'd chosen the rich cream color because it complemented the hint of flame in her brown hair.

He shone the flashlight's beam over the back seat and floorboards, then started to move aside for her to get in. At the last moment, he impulsively blocked her path.

"Brad's having a good time. Don't worry about him."

She let out a small breath that sounded like an attempt at a laugh. "That's easier said than done."

Boone reached up and touched the dark strand of hair that caressed her cheek. He pushed the hair back and took the honor himself, trailing his fingers over the soft, fair skin. "What can I do to reassure you?"

It was hard to tell what happened next. Did he pull her to him, or did she move toward him first and lay her head on his chest? It didn't matter. What mattered was that she was finally where she belonged ... in his arms.

He held her, but not so tight she'd pull away. His touch was gentle, even lighter than he'd used when rescuing the kitten. He didn't want to scare her away, not when she'd finally allowed him to be strong for her.

Years ago, he'd wanted to be her protector. He'd wanted to take care of her the way she tried to take care of others. Nixie had so much love to give, and he wanted her to share it with him. But she'd been so busy trying to be the strong one—the one who visited the elderly at the retirement home, who tutored the slower learners, and who organized fundraisers for the less fortunate.

Now, fifteen years later, she was still trying to be the strong one—for her children, in her business, and for her rescue victims. He wanted to show her she didn't have to be strong all the time. She could be vulnerable ... and soft ... and feminine. Boone's hands moved over the baggy windbreaker that covered her slight frame.

She lifted her face to look at him.

In the warm glow that shone from the car's interior light, he saw the fear in her eyes. He suspected the fear came not so much from concern over her son's well-being, but from the knowledge that she could not protect those she loved from the dangers of everyday life. She was afraid of not being in control.

He lowered his head and touched his mouth to the sweet lips that had taunted him since his youth. The lips that had grown fuller, redder, and more inviting with time. His hand coursed down to the small of her waist and pulled her closer to him, as if that small action could somehow bring him the satisfaction he needed.

Nixie pressed closer, her body pushing back against his torso in welcome invitation. They shifted, and she was against the car.

He explored the sweetness of her mouth with his tongue. It was as if they couldn't get close enough to one another. But if they got any closer, there'd be no turning back. Boone raised his head and looked down at the woman who seemed to need him as much as he needed her.

Her eyes were heavy-lidded with desire, and her breath echoed in the stillness of the night. Only a moment ago her hands had clutched his shoulders; now they relaxed and rested in a loop behind his neck.

"Wow," she said. "You sure do know how to reassure a person."

He laughed, tightened his arms around her until her feet no longer touched the ground, and turned them both around in a carefree spin. He planted a light kiss on her swollen lips. "If you don't go home now," he warned, "we're going to end up spending the whole night out here. And I don't think Brad or Alonzo would be happy about that."

Nixie moved to get in her car, then hesitated. "Boone?" she said.

He looked at her, knowing that if she didn't leave soon, he'd be tempted to take her in the back seat. And he wanted their first time together to be more special than that. "Yes?"

"Thanks."

He grinned. "Anytime."

"For taking good care of Brad, I mean."

"Sure. That, too."

🌿 8 🐾

Nixie was going to wring his neck. Boone wouldn't blame her if she did. After all that talk about taking care of Brad, here he was bringing her son home in this condition.

Boone flipped down the visor to shade his eyes from the mid-afternoon sun. He glanced over at the boy riding shotgun in the seat beside him. Brad gave him a lopsided grin and started giggling uncontrollably.

"Ish it kinda hot in here?" Brad slurred. He reached for the air-conditioning control and almost toppled over, but he was restrained by the seat belt across his chest.

"I'll get it." Boone cranked up the air conditioner and aimed a vent at Brad. It was bad enough the kid was going home this way. He didn't want him getting sick, too.

Boone scratched the stubble that had sprouted overnight on his chin.

How was he going to tell Nixie her son was drunk?

Minutes later, he was pulling up in Nixie's driveway. Boone wished he'd had a couple of hours to take Brad to his apartment and let him sleep it off before he came home. But Nixie was expecting them, and she'd worry if he wasn't home on time.

He killed the engine and walked around to open Brad's door. The boy was asleep, his cheek resting against the fabric seat belt.

"Come on, Sleeping Beauty," Boone told him. "It's time to own up to our misdeeds."

Brad roused, but only slightly, so Boone scooped him up and carried him toward the house. Just as he'd feared, Nixie saw her son and assumed the worst.

"What's the matter with him?" she demanded. "How did he get sick? Is it food poisoning, sun poisoning, what?"

"Let's get him inside. Then I'll explain everything."

Brad was soon settled on the couch. Boone, Nixie, and Bethany stood in a semicircle around him and watched as he tried to open his eyes and keep them open.

Boone turned to Bethany. "Would you get your brother a bucket, honey? In case he ... you know, barfs."

The girl glared at him, her expression almost as

fearsome as her mother's. "Brad *never* gets sick," she declared and huffed off to get the bucket.

Nixie knelt down and felt her son's forehead for fever. "What happened to him?" she demanded.

"Well, uh...." To stop himself from fidgeting, Boone shoved his hands in his pockets. There was no delicate way of putting it, so he may as well say it right out. "He sorta got a little bit looped."

Nixie stood up stiffly and turned to face Boone. He couldn't remember ever seeing her this angry. Her voice, when she finally responded, was soft but far from gentle.

"My son is *drunk*?"

Brad stirred and said, "We played *shug-lug*."

Nixie turned to Boone. "Shug-lug?"

"He, uh, means chug-a-lug." He grinned as he remembered the silly game they had played before they left camp. "We had a little contest to see who could make the bottom of their juice box slurp first."

Bethany came back into the room and placed the bucket on the floor near her brother.

"Where," said Nixie, "did Brad get alcohol?"

"Brad's drunk?" Bethany turned and gave Boone another evil glare. "Mom," she said, "if he keeps on like this, he'll be in jail by the time he's ten."

Nixie pointed up the stairs. "Bethany, please go to your room."

The girl made a sullen exit. "Why don't you send Boone to his room?" she called down the stairs. "*He's* the one who got Brad drunk."

Boone cringed, but her reaction was understandable. He would have felt the same way if he'd been in Bethany's shoes.

"Why don't we go into the kitchen and talk," he suggested, "while we make him a pot of coffee."

"No fair!" Bethany called down the stairs. "I never get to drink coffee."

Nixie rolled her eyes and followed him into the kitchen. "What did he drink?"

Boone thought for a moment. "Wine cooler, I suppose."

"You suppose? You don't know? Where did he get this wine cooler?"

He reached up and rubbed the spot in front of his ear. "From you."

Nixie almost dropped the coffeepot, and Boone leaped to catch it. She was handling this better than he'd expected. He put the glass pot under the drip mechanism. Walking over to the table, he pulled out a chair for her.

"Remember those juice boxes you sent?" At her affirmative nod, he continued. "One of them had apparently been in the refrigerator awhile and fermented. After Brad started getting goofy, I checked the date on the box. It had expired a long time ago."

He watched the emotions that came and went on her face. She'd gone from anger to disbelief to something that looked like guilt.

"Oh, my gosh," she said, whacking her palm

against her forehead. "That must have been the one that had been pushed to the back of the refrigerator. I thought the box seemed a little puffy, but I was in such a hurry I didn't look at it closely."

"Don't blame yourself." Boone reached across the table to cover her hand with his own. "I should have suspected something when Brad said his juice tasted 'tingly.'"

Nixie sighed heavily and buried her face in her hands. Boone wished there was something he could do or say to make the situation better.

Her shoulders were shaking now. Boone wanted to dry her tears and comfort her, but he didn't. Considering the mood she was in, he wouldn't be surprised if she used that self-defense move she'd threatened him with last night.

Then, to his surprise, he realized that her muffled sounds were actually laughter. Her shoulders shook harder, and she lifted her face until her eyes met his. She wiped a tear from the corner of her eye and giggled again.

"It's so ironic," she said. "I prepared him for snakebites, broken bones, cuts, bee stings, getting lost, and everything else I could think of. Never once did it cross my mind to teach him how to identify alcoholic drinks or what to do in case he drank too much."

Boone got up, poured a cup of coffee, and handed it to Nixie. When she started to get up to take it to Brad, he stopped her.

"No. It's for you. The best thing Brad can do right now is sleep. Here." He passed the sugar for her coffee. "You need it more than he does."

He poured himself a cup and joined her.

"There's no way you can anticipate everything," he said. "All you can do is exactly what you've already done ... prepare him the best way you know how, then pray he'll have the good sense to use what you've taught him so that he can take care of himself."

Nixie ran a finger around the rim of her cup. "It's so hard, wondering if the things I try to teach him actually sink in. He's so ... giddy sometimes."

"You don't have anything to worry about," Boone assured her. "He wasn't giddy when he was treating Alonzo's bee sting, was he?" She shook her head, and he continued. "And he wasn't giddy this morning when he cooked his own eggs over the campfire."

She sat upright, and her spoon clattered on the table. "You let him near an open fire?"

"Yes, and his eggs looked so good I asked him to make some for me." He realized it was difficult for her to loosen the apron strings, but for Brad's sake she must. "He's going to grow up whether you like it or not. Wouldn't it be better to supervise him when he tries new things than to keep denying him and take a chance that he'll sneak behind your back to do it?"

She didn't respond, but Boone knew he'd given her something to think about.

"Why don't you go try to sober Brad up, and I'll dilute some coffee with milk and take it to Bethany."

"I don't let the children drink coffee. Except when they're drunk," she amended. "The caffeine's bad for them."

Boone flashed her a winsome smile. "If I were you, I'd make an exception this time. Unless, of course, you want her thinking she has to get potted in order to sample it."

Upstairs, Bethany didn't have much to say—just sat there on her bed, sipping coffee—so he chatted about a little of this, a little of that. She answered his questions with a nod or shake of the head. Anything else he asked was met with a sullen shrug. It was only when he mentioned the new kitten, Stormy, that she gave him more than a one-word response.

"Stormy is an intruder in Precious' domain," the girl said, quoting her mother. "He has to be kept in the utility room to keep from being attacked." She paused a moment as if something had just occurred to her. "There are enough animals in this family for us to love. We didn't need any more."

Boone had a suspicion she was talking about human animals, too, but he didn't take the bait. "If you don't want Stormy, I can put an ad in my paper and try to find him a new home."

She looked up from her cup. "Mom said we should wait a while to see if Precious will learn to accept him. But I don't think she will," she added fatalistically. "Precious knows I love her, and she doesn't want to share me with anyone else."

Boone stood and patted the girl on the knee. "Give her some time. She'll come around."

As he left the room, he saw that she was shaking her head. Was she referring to Stormy or to herself?

Downstairs, he found that Brad was up and around. The boy was standing by the bird cage, burping for all he was worth. The bird roamed free on top of the cage and seemed more than mildly interested in the strange noises coming from its owner. Nixie strode into the room with another cup of coffee and handed it to her son.

"If you're going to teach Tarzan to burp," she told the blond-haired rascal, "at least teach him to say 'excuse me' afterward."

Neither had seen Boone descend the steps. He stood at the bottom, leaning against the curved handrail, watching them ... and enjoying what he saw. This family obviously loved each other, accepting the personality quirks of each without question. Boone liked that Nixie didn't try to shame her son into using better manners. She merely accepted that he was being playful, and she was willing to compromise.

That attitude was totally different from his ex-wife's. Cheryl had come into their marriage with expectations that opposed Boone's in almost every way. She hadn't wanted children, for instance. That was the big one.

As for the other things, Boone probably could

have lived with them. Such as her compulsion about having a spotless house at all times. He'd never forget the time he tracked in mud after a touch football game with the neighborhood teens. Or the time he suggested they go canoeing. She'd just had her hair and nails done, she reminded him, and she had no desire to wallow in a dirty river with fish and bugs and snakes.

Even that he could have lived with. But they both knew their marriage was doomed the day he brought home half a dozen Scouts for their first weekly den meeting. He'd been so excited about starting a Scouting group where there had previously been none, and he was enthusiastic about making a positive impact on the young lives.

When he'd explained to Cheryl how much Scouting had helped him grow emotionally and become more confident, he'd been sure she would accept their presence for an hour and a half each week.

But she hadn't. While Boone was still glowing over the success of his first den meeting, Cheryl had insisted that he not bring "those noisy little brats" back to their home.

And now, here was Nixie, tolerating her son's disgusting noises with an amused smile. This was a close and loving family, and Boone wanted to be part of it.

After his conversation with Bethany, though, he knew he'd have to tread softly.

He stepped into the living room. "Are you feeling better, Brad?"

"A little. Mom said the juice must not have been very potent if I bounced back this quick." He put emphasis on the word *potent,* as if he liked using what he considered an adult word.

"Glad to hear it," Boone said and smiled at Nixie. He was also glad to see that she smiled back at him. Maybe she wouldn't hold the incident against him after all.

"Hey, Mom," said Brad, "can I cook my breakfast tomorrow morning? Boone says I make some mean scrambled eggs."

She glanced again at Boone before answering. "We'll see," she said noncommittally.

"And Boone has this Scout pin that he's had since the olden days when he was a kid!"

"It's not exactly antique," Boone said with a grin, "but it is old. Here, you can wear it until I leave, if you want. Just don't lose it." He took it off and handed it to the boy, who turned the metal ornament over in his hands and admired the piece.

"I'm going to take Tarzan up to my room," he announced. "He likes to play with my toys." And then he was gone.

Nixie watched her son's departure. He took the steps a little more slowly than usual, but she was relieved to see that he hadn't been strongly affected by the fermented juice. She would have never forgiven herself if he'd had more than the mild reaction he'd suffered.

When she turned her attention back to her guest, she was unnerved to find him studying her. She wondered if he thought Brad was crude for burping at the bird. It must certainly reflect poorly on the way she was bringing up her son. And Boone certainly had opinions about other areas of the boy's upbringing.

"He's not usually that rude," she ventured. "I do teach the children good manners."

"It shows," he agreed. "They're good kids."

Nixie looked up at the handsome man who was now absentmindedly jiggling the bell hanging from Tarzan's cage. She wasn't surprised that her son was fond of him. She worried, though, that Brad might become too attached to him and get hurt. After all, there was no guarantee that he'd stay in Bliss. Or even that he wouldn't meet someone nice, fall in love, get married, and have a family of his own.

For some inexplicable reason, that last thought made her uneasy. If he did get married and drop out of their lives, Brad wouldn't be the only one hurt.

Nixie was amazed at how quickly Boone had found a place in their family ... and in their hearts. She had always been fond of him, even when he had tormented her with his endless teasing. And though she tried to deny it, she'd missed him when he moved away from Bliss after graduating from high school.

Maybe that was why she'd fallen so head over heels for Paul and married him shortly after they'd finished school. Her friends had told her Paul reminded them of Boone. She hadn't seen it then, but now she finally admitted that her husband's blond good looks and his gentle teasing were what had turned her head. The very qualities that had annoyed her in Boone.

To her, it had seemed as though Boone's looks were merely a tool for attracting girls, for he certainly must have had a black book chock-full of names. And although his teasing had been tiresome at the time, it had pleased her to be the focus of his attention.

To be truthful, Nixie liked having Boone back in her life. Although he still frustrated her with his joking and needling, Nixie found that she was becoming less resentful of his intrusion into the family's affairs and more eager to see him during his frequent visits.

Not that she was taking his overtures too seriously. She was well aware that even though he'd practically knocked her socks off last night, it had most likely been little more than a mild flirtation to him.

Even so, she couldn't keep from blurting out, "Bethany's ballet recital is next Saturday. Would you like to come along?"

Boone let go of the bird's toy. "Me? Go to Bethany's ballet?"

"If you're not interested, that's okay. I just thought I'd ask." She should have known better than to ask a jock to accompany her to a children's ballet recital.

"I'm interested," he quickly asserted. "It's just that Bethany seems a bit out of sorts with me. I don't know if she'd want me there."

"Don't mind Bethany. She's just gearing up for her teenage rebellion."

"Then I'll be there with bells on."

He smiled, and the simple gesture warmed Nixie to her toes.

If she'd had even the slightest inkling that their kiss beside the car had meant something to Boone, that thought was thoroughly dispelled the next week when he showed up with three more "applications."

This time she didn't leave the room but stayed and acted interested in seeing who wanted to court her. If Boone could kiss and forget, then she would, too. Or, at least, pretend to.

"Change your mind about meeting someone through a personals ad?" Boone asked as she sat on the couch beside him. Brad was perched on his knee, and Bethany sat close enough to scan the printed emails over his shoulder as he read them aloud.

"Curious," she responded, "just like you and the kids."

He gave her a sidelong look that let her know

quite clearly he was suspicious of her change in attitude.

"Come on," Bethany urged. "Read."

"Yeah," Nixie prompted. "The man of my dreams could be in one of those emails."

When he took his time unfolding the first, Nixie snatched the small bundle from his hand. "We don't have all year. I'm not getting any younger, you know." She grinned to see the surprised look on his face. "If I'm going to meet these guys, I want to do it before I'm an old maid."

She cleared her throat and began reading the first letter. It rambled at length about his career and hobbies. Not exciting, but not a turnoff, either. It ended, "I'm a firm believer in marriage. My third wife left me last month, and I want to try again."

"Well," Boone piped up, "he certainly has plenty of experience for the job."

"Experience at being a husband," Bethany said. "But does he have experience at being a daddy?"

Brad grabbed the letter and balled it up, mimicking Boone's action from the last time. "I vote no on this one."

Thank goodness! Nixie had been half afraid her son would overlook the man's failure at marriage in favor of his interest in car racing.

The next two were no better. One said he thought animals were great, but since he was highly allergic, they would have to stay outside. That was enough to dissuade the children from considering him a possibility.

The last one wanted to know Nixie's career and income level. He had accrued some debts and reasoned the best way to pay them off would be to add another paycheck—Nixie's.

Nixie carried the letters to the trash can and dropped them in. She'd been relieved that all the letter writers had obvious flaws. Even though she'd pretended an interest in learning about the candidates, she would have had a hard time explaining to her children why she wouldn't want to meet a stranger who happened to fit their qualifications.

Coming back to the den, she reminded her family that this was the reason she'd been against the idea of the ad in the first place. "Anyone who's good enough to be your daddy is probably already taken," she added. "Now let's go. Uncle Jay and Aunt Lauren are going to meet us at the restaurant before the recital. We'd best not keep them waiting."

As it turned out, Boone, Nixie, and the children had to wait for Uncle Jay and Aunt Lauren. Boone made the waitress giggle when he asked for a child's placemat for himself, then colored the cartoon characters and worked the math puzzles with the children. They seemed to enjoy having him join their fun, and Nixie was pleased to see that Bethany had dropped her sullen attitude. Nixie was glad she'd talked her daughter into wearing the ballet-slipper necklace Boone had given her. He'd noticed it right away and commented how it couldn't do justice to her own sparkling beauty.

The Thomases had come to this restaurant before, but with Boone here, their group now seemed complete. It would have been like this if Paul had lived, Nixie thought.

With a small shake of her head, she realized it wouldn't have been the same. Paul had stayed so busy with work, he had seldom made time for family outings. She wondered if they would still be married now. Would the tiny hill of dissension his worka-holism had created in their marriage have eventually grown into a mountain too tall for either to overcome?

She looked across the table at Boone sitting hunched over the paper placemat. His every move was being copied by Brad. He must have noticed it, too, for he stuck his tongue out one side of his mouth as if in concentration. Brad copied that. When Boone picked up his glass of soda and took a sip, Brad reached for his milk and stopped.

"Milk is for babies," he told Boone. "Mind if I have some of yours?"

"Sure," Boone told him, passing the glass. "Just don't get any backwash in my drink—"

Brad grinned and put the glass to his lips.

"—because I don't want it mixing with *my* backwash."

The boy sputtered, and lemon-lime soda went down the front of his shirt.

"Psyched you out," Boone said and handed him a napkin.

Nixie and Bethany handed over their napkins, as well. They shared a look that only mothers and daughters understand. Nixie looked up to find Boone watching them.

"What?" he asked. "At least we weren't playing gross-out."

Bethany giggled. "Last time we played that, Mom sent us to our rooms. She said it's dangerous to laugh while you're eating because you could choke. Right, Mom?"

Before Nixie could answer, Uncle Jay and Aunt Lauren joined them, filling the remaining two seats at the table.

The waitress took the food orders for all of them, and Nixie was surprised to see Bethany take off the satin-slipper necklace and tuck it into her purse.

What was worse, Boone had seen it, too.

9

The evening went downhill after that.

When the waitress had asked Brad if he wanted his chopped steak cooked medium like his father's, Bethany had loudly corrected her, saying their father was in heaven. Brad, on the other hand, had reveled in the mistake. Then Bethany had clung to her uncle's hand and made it clear she wanted nothing to do with Boone.

As the evening wore on, it got so bad that when Nixie went backstage with her later to help with her costume, she gave her daughter a firm chewing-out. She doubted that the talk did any good.

Nixie couldn't understand why Bethany, who was normally so pleasant and cheerful with everyone, would so openly reject Boone.

When Boone drove them home after the recital, Brad wouldn't stop chattering and trying to monopolize his new mentor's attention. Nixie worried that her son had an enormous case of hero worship. What would happen when he found out that Boone, like all men, had his own shortcomings?

Goodness, Nixie thought, it would be so much easier if both children would react the same. Then she'd only have to find one solution rather than two.

"I apologize for Bethany's behavior," Nixie told Boone after her daughter had unceremoniously dumped the beautiful long-stemmed red rose he'd given her onto the couch and run into the kitchen to put her other rose— the pink one Uncle Jay had given her—into water. "I don't know what's gotten into her. She's never acted this way before."

"Don't apologize," Boone said. He gave her a one-armed hug. "All these years it's been a tradition to have her family watch her perform. It must have felt weird to have an outsider tagging along."

Nixie shook her head. "I just don't understand it. She was fine with you in the beginning. Then something happened, and she changed from Dr. Jekyll into Little Miss Hyde. If this is what she's like at eleven, I'm not looking forward to sixteen."

Boone smiled and took her hands in both of his. The simple gesture was comforting, and he seemed so full of understanding. This was one of those times when Nixie yearned for a partner to share the bad times with her, as well as the good. On days such as this, she envied the married women who had their husbands to share the burden of raising their children properly. As it was now, she could only hope she was doing the right thing.

"If she turns out only half as well as you did, she'll be one lucky lady," Boone said.

Brad came bounding down the steps wearing an oversize T-shirt that served as his sleepwear. "I'll see you Wednesday for den meeting," he said and gave his Scout leader a high five.

"Sure thing, pal." Boone turned loose of Nixie's hand and took a couple of playful punches at the boy. "Before I forget it again, why don't you run and get my Scout pin?"

The look Brad gave him was one Nixie was well familiar with. He'd worn it the time he made a fake volcano and got baking soda all over the living room. He'd given her that look when she'd been looking for the gauze to bandage a scrape on Bethany's arm and he told her he'd used it all to dress up as a mummy. And he'd used the same expression when his teacher had called to tell her Brad had completed his homework assignment of learning five new words and their definitions from the dictionary but that they'd all been slightly naughty words.

The look now was one of guilt. Nixie's heart lurched. She hadn't thought the evening could get any worse, and now she was being proven wrong.

"Did you break Boone's pin?" she asked.

He shook his head. "I can't find it," he whispered.

Although the boy frequently got into mischief, he was always truthful about his misdeeds. Now, however, he seemed different, subdued even. Nixie couldn't help wondering what else was going on that he wasn't telling.

"I don't know where it is," he mumbled.

"Then I suggest you go upstairs and find it." Nixie turned him around and gave him a little push.

"Don't be too hard on him," said Boone. "It'll turn up."

She wondered whether to voice her fears to Boone, then decided he might be able to help her deal with Brad if she was able to point out the problem. Then again, he might just laugh away her concern and suggest she was overreacting as she had the night she'd gone back to the camporee. She took the plunge on the off chance he might be able to help her deal with the situation.

"I think it's wonderful how Brad looks up to you. It was cute how he kept copying you this evening," she began. Boone's answering smile was quick. "But I'm worried that he might be obsessed with the idea of being just like you. It seems like he's carrying this mentor thing too far."

Boone's proud smile turned downward into a perplexed scowl. "What's your point?"

Nixie swallowed. The last thing she wanted to do was hurt his feelings, especially after all he'd done for Brad's confidence. And she didn't want to heap another insult on top of those thrown by Bethany this evening.

"You've been a terrific influence on Brad. The

teacher said he'd settled down at school and is less disruptive, and he doesn't tease Bethany as much as he used to."

"But?"

Nixie turned away from him as she thought about how to phrase what she had to say. "I'm worried that Brad is developing an unhealthy attachment to you." She turned to face him and saw that his features were rigidly composed. "He's so obsessed with emulating you that I suspect he may have taken the pin because he wants so much to be like you."

"Has he ever stolen anything before?"

"No, but—"

"Then it seems you may be jumping to conclusions."

He was angry, and Nixie had only meant to solicit his help. She'd really managed to stick her foot in it this time. "I've seen that look of his before. I know when he's hiding something."

"Then why didn't you ask him instead of accusing him?"

"Because," Nixie blurted, pushing her hair behind her shoulder, "I made the mistake of thinking you might be able to help me."

A cat yowled upstairs. A moment later, Bethany came thumping down the steps with Stormy in her arms. She ran past them, went through the kitchen to the utility room, and locked the little creature in.

"It's not going to work, Mom," she declared as she stomped back into the room. She shot a guarded look at Boone before continuing. "Precious doesn't want anyone else in our family. Everything was just fine before the new guy showed up."

Tears threatened to spill from her eyes.

Nixie opened her arms and pulled Bethany to her. The child's dark-blond hair fell against Nixie's shoulders. She would be tall, like her father, Nixie thought inanely.

Strange how she'd been thinking of Paul more often lately. She wondered if it had anything to do with Boone's presence in their lives. At the oddest times, she found herself comparing Boone to her late husband.

She looked up to see Boone backing away.

"I guess I'd better go now. Let me know if you want me to find Stormy another home."

Nixie hated to see him go home on this sour note. She wanted to apologize for the rotten evening. She wanted to thank him for being a good sport. She wanted to walk outside with him and kiss him good night. Instead, all she said was, "Thanks, I'll let you know."

He gave Bethany's hair a light tug, then hollered up the stairs to Brad. "Be ready for den meeting on Wednesday. And keep looking for that pin."

It seemed as though the minute he was gone, Bethany's tears dried.

"Don't worry about Stormy," Nixie told her daughter. "I'm sure he'll find a welcome place in our family before long."

Bethany scowled. "I wouldn't count on it."

When Boone arrived Wednesday evening, Tarzan was screeching at the top of his lungs. The sound effects were enough to rival any Amazon jungle movie.

"What's the matter with him?" Boone yelled over the din. He approached the cage with a finger in each ear and stared curiously at the noisy beast.

"He's mad because Brad won't take him out of the cage," Nixie said.

"Aw, Brad, let the little guy out," Boone urged.

"But, Boone, he'll plop on my Scout shirt."

Nixie watched as Boone released the bird-proof latch and let the loudmouth out of his cage. Tarzan moved from Boone's finger and sidestepped up his forearm. The bird lifted his scaly feet high as if the hair on Boone's arm tickled them, then he bent over and teased one of the hairs with his beak.

"He's not used to furry arms," Brad said when Boone chuckled.

Boone leaned over and whispered something to Brad. When her son's face clouded and he shook his head in the negative, Nixie knew Boone had asked about the pin. They had turned Brad's room upside down looking for the memento but had been unsuccessful in the search.

Just as she'd suspected they would.

"I'll go look one more time," the boy said and dashed upstairs.

Bethany was in the kitchen loading the dishwasher. Nixie had been surprised when she'd volunteered to handle the job just as she heard Boone's car pull up in the driveway. The girl's animosity must be high if she preferred doing the dreaded dishes over spending time in his company.

"Excuse me a moment," Nixie told Boone. "I have to get some money to cover Brad's Scout dues." She left him talking to the bird.

When she came back, he was still talking to the feathered mimic in a hushed tone.

"If you talk quietly when you're teaching him a word, he'll only repeat it in a whisper," she mentioned.

"What makes you think we're not having a conversation?" he asked. "Tarzan's been telling me about his recent discoveries of how to achieve increased aerodynamics."

"Don't let him fool you," Nixie warned with a teasing grin. "Tarzan's just repeating what he and Brad discussed last night. That bird doesn't have an original thought in his head."

The smile he gave Nixie stirred her in a way she couldn't remember ever feeling before. It was a smile of appreciation and humor that made Nixie feel as if she'd just made the wittiest remark in the world. It made her feel brilliant, unique, and ... special.

She gazed back at the man who made her feel this

way. What was it about him that turned her emotions upside down? In high school he'd caused her blood pressure to rise with his relentless heckling. And now he was giving her heart palpitations with a mere look. If she wasn't careful around Boone Shelton, she might be one of the next rescue victims for her squad. She just hoped it wouldn't be because of a broken heart.

Boone was the first to break the soft silence that had grown between them. "Your kids are going to think they've hit the jackpot today." He patted the papers in his shirt pocket. "They received an all-time high of four applications to choose from."

Nixie's jaw went slack, and she firmly clamped it shut. She felt so off-balance she reached for the wall to steady herself. A minute ago, he'd been making eyes at her that said, in no uncertain language, he had tender feelings for her.

Could they have been the kind of tender feelings someone has for a friend? Her mind raced. No. That kiss they'd shared the night of the camporee assured her otherwise.

Brad returned from his room, giving Nixie a moment to gather her jumbled thoughts. He shrugged at Boone, his lips pressed into a thin line.

"Don't worry," Boone told him. "You'll find it soon. Just keep looking."

Nixie came back to reality with a snap. She supposed it was possible Brad had lost the treasured Scout pin. But he swore he hadn't left his bedroom with it, and the three of them had hunted in, around, and under everything in his room. Maybe it would turn up soon. She hoped so, even if it meant proving Boone right. Knowing Boone as she did, she wouldn't put him above an "I told you so."

Boone handed the envelopes to Brad, who immediately called his sister into the room.

Once again, they settled themselves onto the sofa to peruse the letters, and Nixie felt an ache in the pit of her being. She had thought there might be something special between them, but here he was, excitedly screening daddy candidates with her children. She couldn't bring herself to join them as she had done last time, but some morbid sense of curiosity forced her to stay.

She flopped down into the chair beside Tarzan's cage and picked up a magazine. Flipping through it, she found a list of "Ten Sure Signs Your Man Is Right for You." Maybe she should give it to the children to use as a checklist.

Boone sat with a child on either side of him. He was crazy about these kids and wished he could apply for the job they'd advertised. But he'd already caused enough problems for them. Although he didn't like to think it was so, there was a slight possibility that Nixie was right about Brad going overboard trying to imitate him. And then there was Bethany who, for whatever reason, had decided she wanted nothing to do with him.

He glanced up at Nixie. It was obvious she was pretending to read that magazine. He couldn't blame her for sitting on the other side of the room, away from him. Not after his high school reaction to the feelings that had passed between them. Why hadn't he simply told her she was beautiful instead of bringing up the latest batch of applicants?

Boone ripped open the first envelope. He hadn't told her she was beautiful, he reminded himself, because it was hard to say that kind of thing when the mere thought paralyzes your lips and squeezes your lungs until you can't breathe.

He took a deep breath and read the first one out loud. It was a well-composed, thoughtful letter that portrayed the sender as an intelligent, caring person.

"Hey, you can't beat this one," he told the children. "This guy even put a couple of Bible verses at the bottom of the letter. Proverbs 13:24 and Ephesians 5:23."

Nixie looked up. Boone just smiled at her as Brad raced Bethany to the bookshelf to get the Bible.

Bethany found the first verse and read it. "'He that spareth his rod hateth his son: but he that loveth him chasteneth him betimes."

"What does that mean?" Brad asked.

Boone smiled again. "It means this applicant is in favor of corporal punishment."

The boy's eyes grew large, and he put his hands behind himself as if to protect his rear. "Nobody's going to punish my corporal!"

"Let's see what the other verse is," Boone urged.

Bethany read again, her voice strong and clear.

"'Ephesians 5:23. For the husband is the head of the wife, even as—'"

"I vote no on this one," Nixie interjected.

"Then it's unanimous." Bethany ripped the letter into small pieces and placed them on the sofa beside her.

Like a tiny green hawk, Tarzan swooped down on the paper bits, nabbed one, and carried it back to his cage.

Boone sneaked a peek at the next letter and chuckled. "If you didn't like the last one," he told Nixie, "then you probably won't like this one, either."

She looked up from watching the bird play with the paper. "Let me guess. He's a man of the nineties. The eighteen-nineties."

"You've got it! This guy says he believes most women today are too uppity and don't know their place. He wants someone whose only career would be keeping his house clean and cooking his meals."

In answer, Nixie shook open the magazine and put it in front of her face.

"Since you didn't like that one," Boone persisted, "maybe you'd like *this* guy's sense of adventure." The magazine came down a few inches until Nixie's eyes showed above it. "He's moving to Alaska soon and doesn't want to go alone."

"No," Brad insisted. "Tarzan's a jungle bird. He wouldn't like it there."

The magazine went back up.

Boone chuckled again, and Nixie's face burned.

As she recalled, they had gone through three letters so far. That meant there was one more, and then Boone would leave for the den meeting. To take her mind off Boone and what he was doing, she tried to focus on the words in front of her. That was when she realized why Boone had laughed just now. She rotated the magazine until it was right side up.

"Nixie, darlin'." The masculine voice was deep and smooth and full of innuendo.

She put the magazine down again and found him staring at her, his eyes full of unspoken promises ... and maybe a little bit of mischief.

"What's the maximum number of kids you want?" The way he said it made it seem as if he were offering to give them to her. Right now. Nixie licked her lips. "Uh, maybe three or four, I guess."

As soon as she answered him, she wondered if she was setting herself up to be the target of another one of his jokes.

In an effort to cover her tracks, she added, "But two are plenty. We have lots of love to go around, don't we?" she urged the children.

Boone handed the final envelope to Bethany. "Then you may as well toss this one, too." He turned to Bethany and Brad and added, "He has five children of his own and wants to know if you two are old enough to help watch his young ones."

"I'm almost old enough to babysit," Bethany replied. "But I don't want to do it for free."

Nixie gave a small sigh of relief. Although the

children had received many more replies from the advertisement than she'd ever expected, none had panned out. She was glad she hadn't been put in the awkward position of refusing to go out with any strange men.

A movement near the cage caught her eye. Tarzan was busily tucking bits of paper under the cloth beneath his cage. Nixie looked closer. From the size of the lumps, she guessed he'd been stashing more than paper.

She reached over and lifted a corner of the cloth. Tarzan shrieked and snatched the sunflower seed that had been hidden in the folds.

Next she found a chunk of withered carrot. Cupping her hand, she started collecting the treasures. A peanut, a paper clip, Bethany's hair barrette...

Tarzan cocked his head and watched while she stood and proceeded to the other side of the cage.

Precious walked through the room, diverting Tarzan's attention for a moment. He gave a full-volume bark, then laughed maniacally when the yellow cat shot past into the next room.

...red building block, Nixie's gold shoulder-duster earring, the plastic ball with the bell inside that Bethany had insisted she buy for Precious....

"What are you doing?" Brad asked.

"Going on a treasure hunt." She handed Bethany the key to her diary, gave Brad the small toy car she found, and returned a miniature wooden apple to its rightful place in the decorative basket atop the television. "Your bird is a kleptomaniac."

Feeling three pairs of eyes upon her, Nixie turned to face them. Their expressions told her they had the same idea. In another moment, they were all searching the folds of fabric beneath Tarzan's cage.

"I found a quarter," exclaimed Bethany. "Finders, keepers."

Brad held something between his thumb and forefinger. "Eww, and I found a bobby pin."

Suddenly, Boone's searching hands stopped as he uncovered the object of their attention. Slowly, as if he were a prospector who had just discovered gold, he lifted it for all to see. Other than a slight curve in the metal post, the pin appeared to be undamaged.

Nixie's eyes left the cherished Cub Scout pin and met his blue gaze. There was no "I told you so" in his expression, just relief. Nixie, on the other hand, was gripped with guilt. How could she have suspected her son of taking the pin? Ever since Boone had come back into her life, she hadn't been thinking straight. Why else would she suspect Brad of behavior that was so out of character for him?

Why was her world so topsy-turvy lately? Even her sleep was often disrupted with images of clear blue eyes and shaggy blond hair. And in her waking hours those same blue eyes were turning her insides to mush.

After straightening the metal post that Tarzan had obviously bent with his strong hooked beak,

Boone turned to Brad and secured the pin above the boy's pocket.

"You were due to receive this at tonight's den meeting, but considering the circumstances, I'm going to present it to you now." He solemnly shook Brad's hand. "Congratulations on making such progress with the projects in your Cub Scout manual."

Nixie smiled with pride at her young man. Quickly she hugged Brad before he could resist the "icky" show of affection.

Turning her attention back to Boone, she said, "Thank you for your understanding." She wanted to say more, but what else was there? *Thanks for believing in my son when I didn't?*

Brad fingered the pin that had grown dull over time. "Awesome, man! Thanks."

Boone squeezed the boy's shoulder. "Looks like you have cause to celebrate, my man. When I earned that pin, my mother drove my sister and me over to Blowing Rock, and we spent the day at Tweetsie Railroad. We could make it a tradition and take you there on Saturday."

The North Carolina amusement park was a four-hour drive away, which would require an overnight stay. At every turn, Boone was embedding himself deeper and deeper into their lives.

Brad turned to Nixie. "Yeah, and when my son earns his first Scout pin, I can take *him*. Right, Mom?"

At every turn, Boone was becoming more firmly wedged into her life. But there was no way she could deny her son, especially after her brief lack of faith in him. "Sure, honey." To Boone, she added, "But first we'll have to figure out the logistics."

But how could she calculate the logistics of protecting a heart?

❧ 10 ❧

Boone got out of the car to fill it up with gas, and he tossed his wallet to Brad in the back seat. "Here, pal. Dig out a twenty for me, will you?"

Nixie watched from the front seat as Brad poked around for the bill. He seemed proud to have been chosen for the task, and Nixie instinctively knew it was Boone's way of showing his trust in the boy. He wanted Brad to know he had complete faith in him, and he was giving him an opportunity to prove his trustworthiness.

It was times such as these that made Nixie feel overwhelmed by the responsibility of being both mother and father to her children.

Brad handed Boone the twenty and continued to look through the wallet. He looked up and caught Nixie watching him. "I'm just looking at the pictures."

When Boone returned, Brad asked, "Who is this pretty lady with the blond hair?"

Nixie felt herself stiffen. He'd always been partial to blondes in high school. She didn't want to hear about his conquests, past or present. "Brad, maybe you should give Boone his billfold back."

"That's okay." Boone pulled out into traffic and eased back in his seat. "It's my sister, Ellen," he told Brad. "I think she's pretty, too."

"Oh," he said. "Then I guess this old lady is your mother?"

"Brad!"

Boone reached over and patted her hand. "No problem, Nix. I'm sure anyone over fifty seems old to a kid Brad's age."

Her son flipped past to the next photo. "Hey, where'd you get a picture of Mom?"

Bethany, who'd been silent until now, leaned closer to her brother. "Let me see that." She studied it for a moment, then looked at Nixie. "I didn't know you ever looked so glamorous."

Nixie took the wallet that her daughter handed her. The face that stared back from behind the clear plastic protector did, indeed, look incredibly like her.

The shoulder-length auburn tresses were curled and skillfully arranged around the small heart-shaped face. The artfully applied makeup accentuated the wide-apart brown eyes, high cheekbones, and full lips.

It was almost like looking into a mirror, except

the woman staring back at her had a more worldly appearance. There was a hard edge about her that made it seem as though she would take no guff from anyone.

Boone cleared his throat. "Uh, I thought I'd taken that one out. It's Cheryl, my ex-wife."

Today, the sights, the rides, and the food they bought from the vendors at the amusement park should have been enough to distract Nixie's mind from the image of the look-alike woman in the photo.

Instead, for the entire morning she felt like a zombie going through the motions of enjoying their day at Tweetsie Railroad.

During the magic show at the outdoor theater, Nixie wondered if Boone had noticed the similarity when he first met Cheryl. On the Ferris wheel she told herself she was being ridiculous—after all, hadn't she herself married someone whose features vaguely resembled Boone's? On the twirling swings, she mentally argued that their spouses' looks had nothing to do with the reason she and Boone had married them. And as they dressed in period costumes and posed for pictures, she remembered that one of the reasons she'd been attracted to Paul was because of his gentle teasing.

Later, after they'd bought cotton candy, Nixie wondered if Cheryl liked the messy confection. The woman in the photo didn't look the type, she decided. Nixie tore off a hank of the pink candy, popped it into her mouth, and licked the stickiness off her thumb. Nixie also felt certain Cheryl didn't look like the type for whom smiles came easily. And if that were the case, it was no wonder their marriage didn't last. How could it, when she had been teamed with a jokester like Boone?

She strolled with Boone and the children past a small cemetery that was fenced off from the rest of the park. At first, she thought the tiny fence-enclosed area was for show, perhaps part of a setting for a Wild West skit. On closer inspection, she realized the gravestones were real and the newest dates were of the 1900s. The theme park must have sprung up around the cemetery, she guessed.

Boone was leaning against the fence, pointing to the large stone closest to them and telling the children his mother's side of the family was related to the Greenes buried here. "We're also distantly related to the Enzers in Boone, North Carolina," he added.

"Is that where you got your name?" asked Brad.

"Sure is. My parents had only been married about six months when I was born, and my mother was very homesick."

Bethany pulled the last of the cotton candy from her paper cone. "But it takes about nine—" She blushed. "Oh, never mind."

Boone gave her ponytail a gentle tug. "That's right," he said without embarrassment. "She and my father were too young for that kind of commitment. That's why their marriage didn't last."

Nixie stood quietly beside him. He had easily shared a part of his life that many would have preferred to keep private. But without lecturing, he'd used the information to drive home a valuable lesson to the children.

"Anyway, my mother missed Boone—the county— so much she named me after it."

Nixie couldn't resist. "Aren't you glad she wasn't from Charlotte?"

Boone whirled around, raised his hands in monster-like fashion, and came after her. Nixie took off up the hill toward the train that would take them on a tour through a staged setting of Wild West, America. The children squealed behind her with Boone in hot pursuit.

They didn't slow down until they reached the platform. Nixie was breathless as she slid into the seat directly in front of the one her children had chosen. Boone scooted in beside her and grabbed her in a bear hug as they waited for the rest of the passengers to board.

Laughing, Nixie leaned into him. It was a good feeling. As they caught their breath, she relaxed against the hard, warm wall of his chest. Leaning her head against his shoulder, she giggled and whispered, "Or Kitty Hawk?"

He clawed his free hand above her. The laughing

sparkle in his eyes let her know he was enjoying this game. "I'm warning you...."

More than a little curious what "punishment" he had in store for her, Nixie giggled again. "Or Faith, North Carolina?"

Making like a vampire, Boone bent over her and pretended to bite her upper arm.

The sensation sent little goose bumps down Nixie's spine. "Sophia, North Carolina?"

He playfully attacked the round of her shoulder. "Hush!" he said in a feigned accent, "or I vill make you pay zee ultimate price."

Next time he was sure to go for her neck. The lure was too great. "Sapphire, North Carolina!"

As soon as his lips touched her neck, Nixie melted like ice cream on a warm day. She was breathless once again, this time from giddy laughter and the sensations Boone stirred merely by breathing against her skin.

Brad popped over the back of their seat and peered down at them. "How about Bald Head Island?"

Nixie looked up to see Bethany's head appear beside her brother's. "Or *Turkey,* North Carolina!" the girl goaded.

Pulling away from Nixie, Boone growled and lunged for the children, which sent them into fits of giggling.

Nixie sat up straighter and set about composing herself. She watched, amused, as Boone reached over the back of their seat and made wild grabbing motions with his hand.

The movement of the train, as it started, aborted their frenzied play. Boone settled down beside her and hung his arm over her shoulder. He turned toward her and lightly dropped a kiss on her forehead.

"*Eew*, barf-o-rama," she heard Brad mutter behind them.

It had been a long time since she had laughed so freely. For the past eight years, Nixie had been working so hard making sure her family was healthy and happy that she hadn't found the time or energy to let loose like this.

Too late, she wondered what the other passengers must think of their enthusiastic display. Glancing past Boone to the couple seated across from them, she saw a wistful smile on the older woman's face. The husband gazed lovingly down at his wife and took her hand in his. It was clear they were remembering with fondness similar episodes from their own past.

Nixie turned her gaze back to Boone's rugged visage. He was so big and rough-looking that he hardly seemed the type to be cavorting so childishly with her and the kids.

Her thoughts took her back to the older couple. They had obviously spent many happy years together. What, she wondered, did her own future hold for her? Would she have someone special to share a history with? Would it be someone who would make her laugh and keep her from taking life's daily grind too seriously?

Goodness, she hoped so.

Would it be Boone?

She sighed softly. Experience had taught her she shouldn't take him too seriously, either ... no matter how delightfully giddy his touch made her feel.

Besides, he was determined to set her up with some stranger who had nothing better to do than answer personals ads in the newspaper, she thought bitterly.

The train rounded a curve as they made their way through the wooded "frontier" land. The motion gently urged her closer to Boone, and she didn't resist the pull.

It might hurt later, but she couldn't worry about that now. For the moment, it was too pleasant enjoying his laughter and the closeness of his powerful body next to hers.

At the end of the day, they were laughing as they left Tweetsie Railroad and climbed into the sun-heated car. The stifling humidity didn't seem to affect the children's enthusiasm. They recounted the day's adventures while waiting for the air conditioner to cool the interior of the car.

"How about when those Native Americans stopped the train at the pioneer settlement?" said Bethany. "I thought I would die laughing when Mom asked that young brave if the medicine man put those braces on his teeth."

Boone snickered as he buckled his seat belt. "It did sort of ruin the effect."

Nixie lounged back in her seat and crossed her arms in front of her. "Are you saying you bought the blond hair and freckles on that brave?"

He grinned back at her. "Actually, it was the sneakers that clued me in."

"I liked the bird show best," Brad chimed in. "It sure would be great to have a blue and gold macaw like the one that rode the little bicycle."

Boone reached back and patted the boy on the knee. "Sometimes people wish for things they don't have when all they have to do is look in their own backyard."

"If you're talking about Tarzan, we don't let him go outside."

"It's a figure of speech," said Boone. He switched to the passing lane, then picked up where he'd left off. "If you ask me, your bird's much smarter than that macaw. You're just so used to having Tarzan around that you're not aware of how special he is."

"Maybe."

"The same could be said about your search for a daddy," he added significantly.

Startled, Nixie looked up from the stuffed toy turtle she held in her lap.

He gave her a saucy wink. "Could be there's

someone you already know who would make a fine daddy."

Nixie touched his arm, silently pleading with him not to raise Brad's hopes. Or hers. "Boone, it's one thing to tease me, but please don't involve the children in your jokes."

"Who said I was joking?"

"Hey, I know!" exclaimed Brad as if a novel idea had just occurred to him. "What about *you*! You already have experience with kids from being the den leader. And you'd suit Mom because you must read a lot if you own the newspaper. Right, Mom?"

"That's a stupid idea if I ever heard one," Bethany butted in.

"It is not!" Brad leaned forward in his seat. "Is he good-looking enough for you, Mom?"

Boone sat up straight behind the steering wheel, batting his eyelashes and flashing his best smile.

What could she do? If she agreed, it would lend encouragement to an unwise pairing. But if she said no to discourage her son, she'd be lying.

Boone had said he wasn't joking. Did he truly think something besides arguing and teasing could come of a relationship between them? Although it first seemed preposterous to her, the idea actually held appeal for Nixie. After all, as much as she tried to deny it, she had come to look forward to his frequent visits.

In fact, she'd been afraid he would run out of reasons to come see them, so she had come up with an idea for a rescue squad fundraiser that would ensure further contact with Boone. She just hadn't told him yet about the upcoming donkey baseball game between the emergency services volunteers and Bliss businessmen.

She looked again at the man who had wedged himself so firmly into her life. The wispy blond hair that reminded her so much of her son's fell in disarray across his forehead. The smiling eyes were so full of humor it was a wonder there was room left over for all that incredible blue. His face, like the man behind it, was strong, straight, and full of character.

As Nixie focused on the rows of even white teeth, she wondered how they'd survived his rough-and-tumble days on the football field. And his lips, narrow and firm, tempted her with memories of their first kiss the night of the camporee. Oh, what wonderful reassurance he had given her.

Her eyes met his, and she realized they held more than humor. They held compassion, concern, and caring. For the first time, Nixie admitted to herself that their kiss had less to do with reassurance than with their feelings for each other.

He was still waiting for her answer. Was he good-looking enough?

"Well, Brad," she began, "when you're choosing a daddy, looks are a lot less important than a person's values and whether he's compatible with the rest of the family."

"Yeah, I forgot about that. You don't believe in corporal punishment, do you?" he asked Boone.

Boone grinned. "For someone like you? I think you're bright enough to reason with. Besides, I plan to build you up on my weight machines. I wouldn't want you getting even with me after you're big enough to punch me out."

"Brad, we need to talk," Bethany declared.

For much of the rest of the long ride home, they whispered furiously in the back seat. It was obvious Bethany was against the idea of including Boone's name on their list of candidates.

Nixie switched on the radio in hopes it would cover their remarks. It wouldn't do to have her children unwittingly insult Boone after he'd been kind enough to treat them to a day at Tweetsie Railroad.

"How about that?" Boone said. "The answer was right there in front of us all along. Isn't it amazing we didn't see it before?"

"I think we need to talk, too." She had to know where he stood on this before he got Brad's hopes up any further—or upset Bethany unnecessarily. As for Nixie, she couldn't bear it if this was another one of his impractical jokes.

Uncle Jay and Aunt Lauren had graciously agreed to let the children spend the night with them so Nixie and Boone could have some time alone. Boone had opened the door on a possibility that Nixie knew neither should be too quick to act upon.

Of course, the children didn't get out the door

without Bethany breaking into tears first. After Brad had told Boone some of the tricks his uncle had played on the family, Boone had suggested Brad remove the batteries from Jay's remote control when he wasn't looking.

At that, Bethany had protested loudly, saying Brad was mean and disloyal to do such a thing to someone who loved them as much as Uncle Jay did. She seemed overly protective, and Nixie couldn't imagine why her normally mild-mannered daughter had become so explosive. She made a mental note to have a long talk with her tomorrow, after Bethany had calmed down. Meanwhile, Aunt Lauren and Uncle Jay could help distract her from whatever had been bothering her lately.

As Nixie assembled a chicken sandwich snack, Boone stayed in the living room, talking to the parrot. She supposed he needed to gather his thoughts, just as she did.

They ate in polite silence. What, Nixie wondered, did one say to a man who has invited himself to become a permanent member of their family?

Boone also seemed thoughtful. She frequently caught him watching her and discovered she liked being the focus of his attention.

While she carried their plates to the dishwasher, Boone fed a bread crust to Tarzan. When she entered the living room, she found him talking quietly to the bird. It seemed he'd had more to say to Tarzan this evening than he had to her.

"We need to figure out where we stand on this daddy issue," Nixie said, "before anything else is said to the children."

Boone nodded his agreement. He tried to put Tarzan back in the cage, but when the bird refused, Boone gave up and let him perch on his shoulder. He followed Nixie to the couch and sat down beside her.

"You already know where I stand," he said. "I thought my suggestion to Brad was a good one. Now we just need to know how you feel about it."

Tarzan leaned forward as if trying to catch Nixie's response.

This was disconcerting enough. She didn't need two pairs of eyes watching her. Nixie folded her hands in her lap and studied them. Nibbling the inside of her cheek, she turned to face him. "In high school, you used to tease me a lot."

He squirmed, then gave her a faint smile. "Yeah, I did, didn't I?"

His reaction let Nixie know he wasn't proud of the torture he'd put her through. "How do I know you're not teasing me again?"

Tarzan lost interest and jumped off Boone's shoulder to climb the Venetian blind cord.

Boone moved closer to Nixie, his very nearness affecting her like a powerful drug, and his blue eyes bored a hole into her soul. "Will this prove how serious I am?"

His arms slid around her. In the next moment, his lips touched hers.

Nixie had replayed their first kiss over and over in her mind, trying to remember and savor the moment in all of its toe-tingling wonder. And now he was actually kissing her again. She felt like the luckiest woman in the world.

This was different from that first kiss. Not as raw and demanding. This time, it was tender and full of promise. That night at the car he'd stirred long-suppressed physical needs within her. Tonight, he touched Nixie's emotional needs.

Nixie had been on her share of dates, and she knew what a man wanted from a woman. But this man wanted her children, too, and that simple fact affected her libido more than any candlelight dinner or expensive champagne could ever do.

When he ended the kiss, he didn't pull away. He was close enough for her to feel his breath on her face. His hand touched hers, and he placed her palm against his chest. Even through the pullover shirt, Nixie could feel the thumpity-thump that surely matched her own heartbeat. His lips brushed hers as he spoke. "Believe me now?"

She smiled and slid her hand up to touch the blond tufts at the back of his neck. "I could use some more convincing."

He kissed her again, this time pushing her down onto the couch, then sprawled beside her. His weight was braced on one elbow, and his left knee lay intimately across the top of Nixie's legs.

"Oh, Nix, I've wanted to hold you like this for so long."

Nixie squirmed with pleasure, and it thrilled her to know the action excited him more. "So, you're saying you want me for my body?"

"I want *you*, Nixie. I want you and everything that is a part of you. Brad and Bethany. Precious and Stormy. Your aunt and uncle. Even this crazy bird that's walking on my back." He kissed her lightly and let his lips trail down to her neck, where he gave her a playful bite. "Do you suppose he'll tell anyone what we've been doing?"

"If you're going to be my children's daddy, what does it matter?"

It had slipped out so unexpectedly. Nixie hadn't consciously accepted the suggestion he'd made to Brad earlier today. It was an intuitive thing, something that had felt so right that she automatically knew it was the right thing to do.

She knew they cared for each other. Though neither had spoken the words, she knew those feelings were love. And she wanted Boone as much as he wanted her.

Boone squinted at the woman who was smiling up at him. If he didn't know better, he'd think she was turning the tables on him with a joke of her own. But he didn't need his glasses to read the expression on her face. It reflected his own feelings. Happiness, contentment ... love.

He wondered how he could be so lucky. He

wondered what he should say. The woman certainly had a way of catching him off guard.

Tarzan sauntered up Boone's shoulder and craned his feathered neck until he looked him straight in the eye. "Can you talk?" the bird asked.

Then, with a whirr of wings and a raucous laugh, the parrot took off for his cage.

"He's right," Boone said. "I'm speechless." His fingers trailed upward along her arm and made circles on her shoulder before blazing a path down her collarbone. She offered no resistance. He drew her closer, tormenting himself further with the desire to have her as completely as a man can have a woman. "So, your answer is yes? You'll let me be Bethany's and Brad's daddy?"

She smiled and returned his embrace, the simple action making him want her more than he'd ever wanted anyone or anything ever before. He'd waited more than fifteen years for her. His patience was giving out.

"If that was a proposal," she murmured against his lips, "it's the strangest one I've ever heard."

They lay cuddled together on the couch, savoring the closeness of one another. No words were spoken, but no words were needed to tell her his kisses and gentle touches had nothing to do with a make-out session and everything to do with claiming each other as their own.

The doorbell rang.

Nixie and Boone froze. Their gazes locked, and

Nixie saw that he seemed as confused as she. When it rang a second time, they both jumped to action, straightening and rearranging their mussed clothes and hair.

Running her fingers through her hair one final time, Nixie answered the door on the third ring.

"What took you so long?" Brad groused.

Standing on the porch behind the children, Aunt Lauren took in Nixie's rumpled appearance. When Boone came behind Nixie and laid a hand on her waist, she said, "Never mind that, Brad. Let's just get Bethany inside so we can tend to her."

"Bethany? What's the matter with Bethany?" Turning to her daughter, Nixie saw immediately what the problem was. The exposed areas of the girl's face and arms were covered with raised, red welts.

Bethany scratched her stomach, then reached down and rubbed her thigh. "I itch, Mama."

Nixie's heart nearly broke at the sight of the ugly hives that covered her daughter's body. The last time she'd had the stress-induced rash was after Paul died. Because Nixie herself had been struggling to cope with the loss of her husband, she'd been unable to comfort Bethany as much as she'd wanted.

Now things were different. She was stronger and better able to cope. Nixie resolved to find and remove the source of Bethany's stress. In the mean-while, she would make her as comfortable as possible.

Nixie urged her family into the house. "Brad, go fill the bathtub with cool water. Boone and Aunt

Lauren, would you sit with her and discourage her from scratching while I get the antihistamine?"

"Want me to put ice in the water?" Brad asked.

"No. Just make it slightly cooler than room temperature."

When she came back, Aunt Lauren had her arm around the girl, and Boone was patting Bethany's hand in an effort to distract her from clawing the rash.

"Here," Nixie said and poured red medicine into a spoon. "This should relieve the itching and swelling." She waited for Bethany to swallow. With a silent wish, she hoped the rash came from an allergy rather than stress. Allergens were easier to avoid and simpler to fix than mental stress. "Did you eat or touch something that might have set this off?"

"Nothing out of the ordinary."

Bethany scratched her neck, and Boone reached up to pull her hand away.

The water stopped flowing in the bathroom, and Brad returned a moment later. "We were just sitting around talking about what we did today. And I told 'em Boone might be our new daddy if you liked him enough."

"That's when the itching started," Aunt Lauren interjected.

Bethany glared at her brother. "You had no business saying that. Especially not to —"

"But it's true! Isn't it, Mom?"

Nixie winced at the sight of Bethany digging furiously at a bright-red welt under her arm. "Never mind that now. Bethany needs to get in the tub."

She led her daughter to the bathroom and sprinkled baking soda in the bath water to help soothe the itching. While Bethany soaked, Nixie went back to the den.

Boone stood as she entered the room. With a sinking heart, Nixie knew that he was the cause of her daughter's distress. But that didn't keep her from hoping there might be another reason for Bethany's hives.

"I'll stay here tonight," Boone told her. Turning to Lauren, he added, "On the couch, of course."

Aunt Lauren nodded.

He took Nixie in his arms and gave her a gentle hug. "I'll stay up all night and look after her if she needs it. And if she's not better by morning, I'll drive her to the after-hours doctor."

For the briefest of moments, Nixie allowed herself to enjoy the feel of her cheek against his chest. She would love to have him spend the night, every night, and not on the couch, either. For now, though, she had to set aside her own wants and put Bethany's needs first.

Reluctantly, she broke the embrace. "That's very sweet of you. But I think it would be better if we kept things as normal as possible. She'll come around more quickly if there's less commotion in the house to upset her."

"And goodness knows she was upset this evening,"

said Aunt Lauren. "I could tell she was agitated, but it really started showing after Brad fooled Jay by taking the batteries out of the remote control. And then when Brad started talking about you two getting married ... well, you know what happened next."

Yes, Nixie knew what happened next. Her daughter had a stress reaction to the mere thought of her marrying Boone.

Maybe she'd be able to ease Bethany's mind about Boone joining the family. But if she couldn't....

As much as she hated having to make the choice, her daughter's health would have to come before her own happiness.

❧ 11 ❧

After church the next day, Aunt Lauren caught Nixie slouched in the overstuffed chair beside Tarzan's cage and reading a romance novel. "Reading more of those love books?" she asked. "Don't you know it's more exciting to participate?" She gave Nixie an impish wink.

Nixie closed the historical saga. "I guess I just needed a happy ending to lift my spirits."

"Bethany still sick?"

"No, she's mostly recovered. She doesn't itch unless she thinks about it."

Aunt Lauren made herself at home on the couch. "Then what's on your mind?"

"I had a talk with her this morning. After some questioning, she admitted she doesn't want me to get involved with Boone."

"It's too late for that, isn't it?"

Nixie gave an ironic laugh. "I think I've been

emotionally involved with Boone since high school. I was just too blind to see it."

"But Bethany sees it, and she's reluctant to share her mother with someone else."

Nixie frowned and rubbed her earlobe. "I don't think that's it. At first, I suspected she didn't want anyone to take Paul's place, but if that were the case, she wouldn't have bought that help wanted ad for a daddy."

Aunt Lauren's sweet face was full of compassion. She was more than just her aunt, Nixie knew. She was her friend. And Nixie was grateful to have such a kind and caring aunt.

"Don't worry, Nixie. It took you a while to get used to Boone, and you finally came around. Bethany will come around, too."

"But that's where I'm confused. It's obvious she's crazy about him, yet she's working very hard to pretend she's not. It just doesn't make sense."

"Most kids don't make sense at that age. Give her time."

Bethany called to them from upstairs. "Mom, you have company."

The front door burst open, and Brad came in, followed by Boone.

"She's upstairs, and she looks normal again," Nixie said.

With a wicked chuckle, Brad added in typical brotherly fashion, "Normal for *her*."

Nixie stood to greet Boone. One look at that

ruggedly handsome face, and she was wishing they were alone again. He smiled at her in a way that made her think he felt the same.

Brad buzzed around his hero like an annoying little gnat. Even so, Boone never broke eye contact with Nixie as he hefted the boy over his shoulder like a sack of potatoes.

"I was worried about Bethany," Boone said. "Brad told me her rash is gone."

"Yes," she agreed. "Our home remedies seemed to do the trick." Nixie failed to add, however, that Bethany's rash disappeared shortly after Boone had left. She hoped the cure had come from her home remedies rather than Boone's departure.

Aunt Lauren stood and joined them. "Boone, we're going to the hospital this afternoon to see Nixie's new niece. Would you like to come along?"

By now Brad dangled upside down as Boone gripped his ankles and pretended to pound him into the floor. "I got a new cousin, Boone. Uncle Ryan and Aunt Francie weren't lucky enough to get a boy like me."

Shifting the boy's ankles to one hand, Boone held his other hand out at waist level and said to Nixie, "Little Ryan has a baby?"

Nixie nodded. "Isn't it amazing how fast kids grow up?" She wasn't referring to her little brother. If only she'd known how quickly she and Boone would grow up and go their separate ways, she may have taken notice of him in a different light. And their lives might have turned out vastly different.

But if that were the case, she wouldn't have had those years with Paul, nor would she have been blessed with these two wonderful children. What really mattered, she knew, was that even though it took them fifteen years to realize it, she and Boone were in love.

Suddenly she wanted more than anything to go to the maternity ward. She wanted to hear those tiny, high-pitched cries and share the joy of new life with Boone.

He turned his attention back to Brad. "Well, don't just hang there," he told the boy. "If you want to see your cousin, you'd better get a decent shirt on."

Later, at the hospital, they dawdled in front of the nursery window and stared at little Merrilee Cordaire. The baby had somehow freed one of her hands from the snug receiving blanket and sucked hungrily on her fist.

"You can tell she's a Cordaire," said Boone.

Nixie looked up at the man standing beside her. "How can you tell?"

"Look how pretty she is."

The look he gave Nixie told her he wasn't talking only about the Cordaire in the bassinet. Nixie took it as a personal compliment, and despite the fifteen years between her and the shy teenager she'd once been, she blushed.

"Gross," Brad said, clutching his stomach. "I'm going to get sick."

Bethany grabbed her brother's hand and started pulling him in the direction Aunt Lauren and Uncle Jay had gone moments before. "Let's go to Aunt Francie's room. After what she went through last night, I doubt she's in the mood to make goo-goo eyes at Uncle Ryan."

Nixie smiled at the sight of her children walking hand in hand down the hospital corridor. Despite their frequent arguments and insults hurled at one another, they were best friends. They just wouldn't admit it. Maybe in a few more years they'd be mature enough to openly acknowledge their affection for each other.

She looked up at Boone. He took her hand and swung it as the children had done when they sauntered away. She squeezed his hand, and he pulled her closer. Maybe that was what she and Boone had needed. Time to mature. They'd been good friends all along, even amid the arguing and the teasing insults hurled at one another. Now they were old enough and mature enough to openly admit their affection for each other.

Boone pressed a kiss on her forehead, then rested his chin against her hair. "Next time we come to this ward, Nixie, I want it to be *our* baby in that bassinet. I was crazy to leave you that first time, and I won't let you get away again." The arm he had slung around her waist tightened with the intensity of his words. "I love you, Nixie. Marry me."

Nixie looked up into the face of the man who had been so many things to her. Adversary, ally, tormentor, friend, and now loved one. Now he was asking to be her husband and the father of her children. If it was only up to her, she'd say yes without hesitation. But just as she did with all major family decisions, she wanted to discuss it with her children first. Her answer to Boone would affect their lives as well as her own.

"There was something in your newspaper's advice column recently that has stuck with me. She makes a lot of sense."

"You mean 'Ask Aunt Alice'?" Boone prompted.

"Yes. She told the person who'd written for advice that when people marry, they don't just join the one they've fallen in love with. They marry that person's family, as well. If you marry me, Boone, you marry my family. And I can't give you an answer without talking to my kids first."

He hugged her. "That's fair. But don't keep me waiting. I can't be patient much longer."

They walked hand in hand down the hospital corridor, swinging their arms in an echo of Bethany's and Brad's action. As they approached Francie's room, they heard laughter.

When Nixie stepped inside, she was surprised to discover Bethany was the only one not joining in on the fun. The girl sat on the empty hospital bed beside

Francie's and stared out the window. Nixie hugged her brother and sister-in-law and sat down beside Bethany.

After Boone shook Ryan's hand and complimented the new mother, he took a seat on the bed, sandwiching Bethany between him and Nixie. Bethany didn't seem happy about it.

For a while, talk centered around Merrilee's birth and Francie's health. Nixie smiled to see the pride that shone on her brother's face. She imagined Boone's reaction would be similar if he were in Ryan's shoes.

Then her thoughts led her into a detailed daydream in which she, rather than Francie, was the new mother. Her parents were due to arrive from Baltimore later this evening, and Nixie imagined them joining the rest of her loved ones in this room to rejoice in the child who was born as a result of her and Boone's love for each other. She wouldn't even care whether it was a girl or a boy, as long as the baby had Boone's good qualities.

"Brad was telling us things are looking pretty serious between you two," said Francie.

Nixie glanced up and caught the look that passed between Aunt Lauren and Uncle Jay. Brad, Ryan, and Francie smiled approvingly. Only Bethany looked glum. Staring down at her hands, the girl refused to join in the conversation.

Boone reached behind Bethany and covered Nixie's hand with his own. "Yes, but Nixie tells me that when a man marries a woman, he marries the family, as well."

Ryan laughed. "You're right. I never realized what I was up against when I married into Francie's family."

Francie gave her husband a playful punch.

Boone shrugged. "Well, I've asked her, but—"

"Boone! This isn't the time or place."

"But, honey, most of your family's right here. You may as well find out right now how they feel about us getting married."

"All for the lovebirds tying the knot," Uncle Jay piped up, "raise your hand."

This was not turning out at all as she had expected. Nixie had planned to have a private talk with Bethany and Brad before announcing their intentions to the rest of the family.

Hands went up, including Boone's, but Bethany stared sullenly into her lap.

"All opposed?" Brad continued.

Everyone turned and waited for the lone hold-out's response. Bethany made an obvious show of concentrating on picking off the remains of her pink nail polish.

"Abstaining, huh?" Boone gave Bethany's hair a little tug. "I'll bet you're just playing hard to get. Right, Steph?"

Nixie was startled speechless when her daughter rose to her feet and stood in front of Boone, hands defiantly on her hips, and declared, "My name is

Bethany, not Steph." Turning to Brad, she added, "And I wish we'd never placed that stupid ad."

Then, wiping the moisture from her eyes, she ran out into the hall.

Nixie didn't know what to do first—apologize to Boone or run after her daughter. And if she went after Bethany, should she comfort her or chew her out?

Although Boone started to follow her, Nixie stayed him with a hand on his arm. "Give me a minute alone with her." She had expected to see the hurt on his face, and it was there. But he seemed more concerned about Bethany's unhappiness. "I'm sorry about the way she's been acting lately. She's not usually like this."

He didn't say anything. Just nodded his under-standing.

Out in the hall, Nixie started to scold her daughter for being so rude, but Bethany had lifted the hem of her shirt to wipe the tears from her eyes, and Nixie's attention was drawn to the bare abdomen covered with hideous red splotches. When Bethany kept rubbing her eyes with the shirt, Nixie pulled the girl's hands away from her face and discovered a large red hive covering most of her right eyelid.

"How long have you been itching?"

Bethany rubbed her eye with the back of her hand, exposing more hives on her wrist. "Since before we got to the hospital. I thought it would go away."

She wriggled her shoulders as if her back itched, too. "Mom, why is this happening?"

Nixie had her suspicions, but if she was wrong, she didn't want to give her daughter any ideas. If, indeed, Bethany was reacting to the stress associated with her unwillingness to accept Boone as her stepfather, Nixie wanted to get to the root of the child's fears rather than hand her an excuse for them.

She hugged her daughter. "I don't know," she said at last. "But we're going to find out why, and we're going to come up with a solution."

Boone took them home, where they repeated the treatment Nixie had used the night before. It was obvious he wanted to help and was frustrated by his inability to do so.

"We should have taken her to the emergency room while we were at the hospital," he said.

Nixie rescued Stormy from another swat by Precious and put the kitten in the utility room. "It's not a life-threatening situation," she told him. "If she has another episode tomorrow, I'll take her to the doctor."

In the end, he reluctantly accepted her decision. He also accepted her refusal to let him spend the night and help take care of Bethany.

Nixie hated sending him away. It meant a lot having someone to share her concern. True, she had Uncle Jay and Aunt Lauren who fussed over the children constantly. And her parents, who were staying at Ryan and Francie's house, would have gladly helped.

But, somehow, it was different with Boone. It was as if their shared concern over the children somehow brought them closer together.

She shook her head at the irony of it. If she was right in her suspicion that Bethany's hives came from her unwillingness to accept Boone into the family, the girl's illness could have the effect of driving them apart.

By morning, the hives had once again miraculously disappeared. When the children got off the school bus that afternoon and stormed into the sign shop, Nixie let Brad play a game on one of the computers while she took Bethany into her office.

Nixie sat beside her daughter on the office couch and studied her carefully. No sign of hives on the exposed skin of her face, arms, or legs. "How have you felt today?"

"Fine."

"Are you itching now?"

"Nope."

Both times Bethany had broken out in the rash, she'd been hearing talk about the possibility of Nixie and Boone getting married. Nixie didn't want to bring on another episode for her daughter, but she had to know what was causing it. And this would be one way to find out.

"You know Boone asked me to marry him," she began.

"So, did you tell him yes? Majority rules, you always say."

No sign of scratching yet. So far, the only thing Bethany was suffering from was a sarcastic mouth. Deciding to concentrate on only one problem at a time, she ignored the tone of her daughter's voice.

"Yes, in most cases the majority rules. Before I give Boone my answer, I want to make sure it's a decision we'll *all* be happy with."

Bethany idly twirled a lock of hair around her forefinger. "Are you saying this time it has to be unanimous?"

"I'm saying I want Boone to be a part of our lives, and I want you and Brad both to accept him as your father." Nixie reached over and pulled Bethany's hand away from her hair. "I love him very much, Bethany, and I want you to be happy for me."

"But it's not right," she cried, withdrawing her hand. "He's not my father, and he can't take anyone else's place."

"No one will ever take the place of your real father," Nixie assured her. "Not for you or Brad, and not for me, either."

"Well, maybe we don't need anyone else in our family."

Nixie wished she could understand what was going on in her daughter's mind. She didn't want to push too hard and make her retreat into a sullen silence. Nixie's voice automatically lowered as when she dealt with frightened patients at rescue calls. "I thought you liked Boone."

"It's not that...." Bethany scratched her cheek,

then started twisting her hair again. "You said that if Precious couldn't learn to accept Stormy, then we should find another home for the kitten. Well, Precious knows there are enough pets in our house. I've been in the family a lot longer than Boone has been around, and I know there are enough people in our house. Why can't you give me the same respect that you give our cat?"

Bethany was near tears, and Nixie tried for a little levity. "You want me to take Boone to the animal shelter?"

It didn't work. Further, Nixie noticed that the spot where Bethany had scratched her cheek was now turning a bright shade of red.

"We're giving Precious and Stormy a chance to work out their differences. The least I can do is give you and Boone the same courtesy." She patted her daughter's knee. "Now promise me you'll give it a try. If things work out as well as I expect they will, you can even be my maid of honor. Isn't that exciting?"

Bethany gave her a listless shrug.

"I knew you'd be open-minded about this," Nixie said, trying for positive reinforcement. But she had her doubts about whether it was working.

That subject handled, Nixie sat Bethany down at the desk to begin her homework and left to tell Brad to get started on his. Then she picked up a job order for a sale flyer and started typesetting it on the computer.

She'd been at it for less than fifteen minutes when Bethany appeared at her elbow.

"Mom, the itching's back, and it feels kind of hard to breathe."

Her eyes were swollen, and she was scratching frantically under the waistband of her shorts.

"Oh, heavens."

Calling out instructions to Uncle Jay, she left him in charge of the shop and asked him to see that Brad got his homework done while she took Bethany to the doctor.

Outside, Nixie fumbled through the first aid kit she kept in the car in a futile attempt to locate some antihistamine. It wasn't something she ordinarily stocked, but she looked again anyway. When she turned up empty handed, she urged Bethany in the passenger side and pushed the speed limit to the doctor's office.

She didn't want to panic Bethany, but a severe case of hives left untreated could cause the throat to swell shut. She had wanted to know if Bethany's hives came from her stress about Boone joining the family. She had her answer, but she wished she had never tried the test.

Not only did she have her answer about Bethany's feelings regarding the marriage, she had managed to set off a bad reaction. Guilt stabbed at Nixie's conscience.

The nurse let Bethany go ahead of the handful of patients sitting in the waiting room. A few minutes later, the doctor gave her an injection, and her breathing soon came easier.

"The swelling should go down within the next hour or two," Dr. Coffman told her.

Nixie motioned him into the hall. "What do you think could be causing these episodes?"

"Well, this is the allergy season, especially for people sensitive to grass pollen. But if she's never had seasonal sniffles before, that's probably not the cause. Perhaps she's allergic to some other substance she has come in contact with."

"Nothing's different other than me dating someone special." Nixie started thinking aloud. "For a while I had this crazy idea she might be allergic to *him,* but today he was nowhere around. Although you know, each time she developed these hives, there had been discussion about us getting married. Do you suppose there could be a connection?"

Their family doctor flipped back through Bethany's chart. "I see that she had hives when she was three."

"Yes, that was after my husband died."

He made a note in the chart, then tucked the pen behind his ear. "Then I suppose it very well could be a case of nerves." Leaving the first pen above his ear, he reached for another from the counter and scribbled out a prescription. "I suggest you keep her calm, and make a note of what she's wearing, eating, touching, or talking about if it happens again." He handed her the prescription.

"And if she has another bad reaction, you may need to inject her with this."

Nixie stared at the scrawled writing on the slip of paper. Just when she was learning to give Brad more freedom without panicking about his safety, Bethany wound up having anxiety reactions.

Why couldn't life be simple?

Over the next couple of weeks, Bethany had a few more reactions, but none were as severe as the first three episodes.

Nixie didn't share with Boone her suspicion about the cause of the rash because she was afraid he might step up his efforts to win Bethany over. And Nixie was afraid the added pressure would only make the outbreaks worse.

As it was, she asked him to give her a while longer before expecting an answer to his proposal. Saying she wanted the children to grow used to the idea of her remarrying, she asked Boone to keep the subject low-key. True to his word, he said nothing else to them about becoming their new daddy.

But his promise didn't keep him from stealing kisses from Nixie when Bethany and Brad weren't looking. And if he didn't have an excuse to stop by and visit, he called to chat, and the phone was usually passed to everyone in the family to say hello.

His good night calls were the ones Nixie looked forward to most. By then, the children were in bed, and they were free to talk without interruption. In the evenings, it felt wonderful to unwind with the man she hoped to marry someday. They were little things—sharing their day's events and laughing about things that wouldn't seem funny to people who weren't in love. And each night Boone whispered "I love you" in the darkness before hanging up.

Such little things, but they meant so much.

Unfortunately, it seemed as though the more firmly Boone rooted himself in their lives, the more frequently Bethany's hives appeared. It was a good thing school was out for the summer because the daily doses of antihistamine tended to make the girl groggy.

"We can't keep going on this way," Nixie told her aunt and uncle when they came to visit one Saturday morning. "It's tearing me up to watch my little girl suffer from these skin rashes. Just when I think she's over it, she'll break out again after Boone calls or if she catches us kissing."

"She's been very clingy to Jay, too," said Aunt Lauren.

Uncle Jay paused in his search through the kitchen junk drawer. "She followed me into the bathroom yesterday. I can't walk through a room without her hugging me and telling me she loves me." He grinned at her. "It's nice to know, but it does get tiresome after a while."

Nixie watched her uncle withdraw a sheet of paper and draw a pair of large eyes on it.

"On the other hand," she said, "Brad has been

teasing her less often and getting into less trouble with his pranks."

Uncle Jay snorted. "That's an improvement? My main man told me it's immature to play a lot of jokes on people."

"Imagine that," Aunt Lauren said dryly. She winked at Nixie.

Jay finished the drawing and headed off toward the stairs.

"Where are you going with that?" she asked.

He stopped and offered up a devilish grin. "Gonna slide it under her bedroom door and make her feel like she's being watched."

Nixie shook her head. "How do you put up with him?" she asked Aunt Lauren.

"You get used to checking whether the bed's been short-sheeted or the toilet seat is greased. It's a challenge to see if I can stay one step ahead of him."

She heard a squeal from upstairs and knew Uncle Jay had scored.

She and Aunt Lauren had each just settled down with a cup of coffee when Boone joined them.

"The door was unlocked," he said in explanation as he helped himself to a cup of the steaming brew.

His inevitable shadow followed him into the kitchen. "What does a man have to do to get some coffee around here?" Brad asked with a mischievous grin. "Get drunk?"

Uncle Jay rejoined them, and he and Aunt Lauren

listened with amusement as Brad told them about the fermented fruit juice.

"What brings you here so early this morning?" Nixie asked after Brad had finished his tale.

"Friends of mine have opened a go-kart track over in Bliss. I thought it would be fun if we drove over and watched some races." He turned to Lauren and Jay. "Y'all come, too. The more, the merrier."

The older couple declined, but Brad raced upstairs to tell Bethany. He came back down after only a few minutes.

"Bethany says she can't go because she's itching again."

Nixie sighed and rose to get the medicine. As much as it broke her heart to acknowledge it, Bethany very obviously was having nervous reactions to Boone's presence. How could she consider marrying Boone if her own daughter couldn't tolerate being in the same room with him?

With a heavy heart, she knew what she had to do.

She turned to Boone. "If you want to take Brad, that's okay with me. I'll stay home and look after Bethany." Then to Aunt Lauren she said, "Would you mind watching the kids after Boone gets back? He and I need to talk."

As much as she hated to do it, she had no choice but to refuse his marriage proposal.

❧ 12 ❧

Boone didn't understand it.

He and Brad had spent a great day at the go-kart track yesterday. The kid was good company, helping keep his mind off of missing Nixie and Bethany. Boone wished they'd been able to come, but he understood that being out in the heat would only make Bethany's rash worse. Yet, he still missed them.

And it prickled at his conscience that he might be the cause of Bethany's hives. She had been keeping him at arm's length lately, and it was obvious she didn't want him to marry her mother.

The confusing part was that, for the most part, she actually seemed to like him. Boone had never had trouble winning over kids before; maybe because he acted like a big kid himself. So why was he striking out with Bethany?

But the really weird part was when Nixie had

blown his socks off with her announcement that they weren't "compatible," and suggested they stop seeing each other. *Hmph*, "suggested" was too mild a word. "Demanded" was closer to the mark.

He'd been such an idiot. While watching the races with Brad, he'd fantasized about being a part of the happy family. He'd daydreamed about sharing the mundane, everyday experiences with the woman he loved and the two children who had found a special place in his heart. He had daydreamed about arguing over whose parents they would visit on the holidays.

And he'd rejoiced in the thought of never having to spend another night alone. It would be such heaven, he knew, to finally claim Nixie as his own. He would claim her with his declaration of love and devotion as he slipped the wedding band onto her slim finger, and he would claim her with his body every night thereafter.

While he'd spent the day thinking she'd planned some private time with him to accept his proposal and finish what they'd started on the couch a while back, she had actually been planning to drop a bombshell on him.

In a way, he was glad he hadn't known what was coming. When he and Brad had bought hot dogs at the concession stand, the matronly attendant had beamed at them both and declared how much Brad looked like his "father." Boone didn't know who was more pleased—he or Brad.

It had been fun to pretend that Brad was his kid.

Yep, he was glad he hadn't known what Nixie was going to hit him with that evening.

Boone reshuffled the papers on his desk and sorted them into stacks. He didn't know why he'd come to the newspaper office today. He couldn't keep his mind focused on his work.

The thing that puzzled him most was that it was plain to see Nixie loved him. She hadn't said the words, but he could see it in her eyes. He'd gone over their conversation in his mind a hundred times since then, and he was convinced it wasn't just wishful thinking on his part. It was plain to see that Nixie wanted him as much as he wanted her.

The only plausible explanation for her refusal of his marriage proposal was Bethany. Why wouldn't Nixie open up and be honest with him? he wondered. Why didn't she realize he could help her overcome Bethany's opposition to the marriage?

He didn't blame Nixie for putting her family first. He probably would have done the same. But he just wished she hadn't handed him that malarkey about not being compatible—that they knew in high school they weren't right for each other and that they were trying to fool themselves now.

Boone ripped open the envelope on top of the stack of incoming mail.

He would be seeing her tonight at his office—a distancing ploy on her part, he was certain—to discuss the donkey ball game she was planning as a fundraiser for the rescue squad. And Boone was determined to use his powers of persuasion on her. He wasn't about to give up without a fight.

Despite her brave words to the contrary, Nixie loved Boone and missed him desperately. She could tell Brad missed his rambunctious friend, too. As for Bethany, she'd turned even more moody and depressed.

Nixie was glad to see the girl's rash disappear. After she'd told the children she wouldn't marry Boone, Bethany had suffered no more hives outbreaks. Nixie had expected the news would cheer her daughter up, but the girl became even more withdrawn.

Nixie was stumped. Bethany, who usually chattered a mile a minute, now spoke in monosyllables. The longest conversation Nixie had heard her daughter conduct these past few weeks had been with Precious, the cat.

They had all decided that since Precious and Stormy couldn't smooth out their differences, the kitten would have to go. Nixie had gone upstairs to put freshly laundered and folded clothes in Brad's room when she heard her daughter carrying on a conversation in her room.

There were no visitors at the house that she might be talking to. Out of curiosity, Nixie laid the clothes on Brad's bed and shamelessly eavesdropped on her daughter in the next room.

"Don't you worry, Precious," Bethany said in her most soothing voice. "We're going to send that bothersome Stormy to live with someone else."

She was quiet a moment, and Nixie guessed she was laying her cheek against the animal's fur just as she'd always done when she needed comforting.

"I wish you could have gotten along with him, because he really is a funny kitten. But I'm your favorite person, and you don't want to hurt my feelings by being friends with Stormy. Do you?" Pause. "Of course you don't."

There was another short silence before she continued her chat with the cat.

"I know just how you feel. Uncle Jay is one of my favorite people—even if he does play tricks on me all the time."

Brad burst into the room. "Hey, Mom! Steven called, and he wants me to come to his house tonight. Will you drop me off before you go to that meeting about the donkey ball game?"

Bethany came into the room, still clutching Precious. "I want to stay with Aunt Lauren and Uncle Jay."

"Sure," Nixie told them. "But you two have swimming lessons in the morning, so we won't stay late."

She said that more for her own benefit than for the children's. Meeting with Boone, as she would be doing tonight, she wanted to limit the amount of time she would spend with him.

She'd felt guilty, lying to him as she had. She knew they were as compatible as two people could be. But she couldn't let Bethany be the fall guy for their breakup. If she'd told Boone the real reason—that Bethany was against the marriage and that Nixie couldn't marry him if it meant choosing between her own happiness and her family's—he would have tried to win Bethany over. And that would have only increased the nervous tension she was suffering from.

Maybe, in a way, she hadn't lied about their compatibility after all. In truth, if Boone wasn't compatible with the entire family, then he wasn't compatible with her.

Nixie just wished the truth didn't hurt so much.

They were going over the final details of their publicity plans for the donkey ball game. Jeff, the rescue worker who had been with Nixie the day Boone had been hit by the car, had agreed to head the committee to find a site for the event and invite local business owners to play for a fee. Nixie and Boone were in charge of publicity, with Nixie making flyers to put in store windows and Boone designing and running public service advertisements as well as a feature article in his newspaper.

Nixie had trouble concentrating on the display ad

spread on the table before them. Instead, she was wondering why she had ever mailed that letter to the advice columnist, "Ask Aunt Alice."

The letter had started as a way for Nixie to organize her thoughts about what was going on between her and Boone. She had hoped that seeing the situation in black and white would help her find a solution to the dilemma she was in. After she had covered both sides of three sheets of notebook paper, she had impulsively addressed an envelope to the *Bliss Gazette's* answer lady and dropped the letter into the big blue mailbox in front of the grocery store.

The minute it had slipped from her fingers and down the mail chute, she'd had second thoughts about sending a stranger such a personal letter. At least she'd had the good sense not to sign her name. She just hoped the columnist wasn't familiar enough with the people of Bliss to connect her name with the return address on the outside of the envelope.

Nixie looked up at Boone as he flipped through online clipart in his search for an illustration of a donkey. It amazed her how the slight motion of sliding the computer mouse could make the oversize muscles in his arm flex and bunch. She longed to lay her hand on his arm, feel the strength beneath her fingertips, and tell him she'd made a terrible mistake when she'd refused his marriage proposal.

But the look on his face was one of businesslike concentration. His whole attitude this evening had been aloof, and his body language clearly said, "Keep your distance."

She didn't blame him. He'd been hurt. Why should he open himself up for more of the same?

"Jeff saved a position for you to play in the donkey ball game," she said. In answer to the empty stare she received from Boone, she added, "It seemed only fair, what with all you've contributed to the planning and advance publicity. The sporting goods store is contributing T-shirts with the names of the businesses represented by each player. You'll need to call them soon to let them know your size."

He just nodded. The only hint of emotion on his face was the jerk of a muscle in his jaw.

Nixie had seen the gesture many times before, but she'd never been the cause of it until now. She had seen it the time a school bully had mocked the slurred words of a partially deaf student. He'd reacted this way when his favorite teacher had told the class she'd been diagnosed with cancer. And then there was the time he'd seen his sister dancing too close to Robert Gage, the ninth-grade heartthrob.

The muscle twitched again in Boone's jaw. "Do you want to use the picture that looks like a nativity scene donkey or the comical one with ears as long as his body?"

"Let's use the comical one," Nixie said, trying to ignore his brusque tone. "It should lure more people to come see the fun."

She wondered how much fun the game would be

if he were still treating her like a business associate. But why should she expect anything different? She was the one who'd insisted she didn't want a personal relationship with him. He was merely giving her what she'd asked for.

There was another hour or so of stilted questions and answers before the rough-sketched ad looked as eye catching as they could possibly make it.

Nixie stood, stretched, and reached for her purse when Boone intercepted her hand with his own.

His voice was so low Nixie had to strain to hear him. "You can't go on pretending."

She pulled her hand back, but he refused to let go. "I don't know what you mean."

"You know exactly what I mean." His eyes narrowed to angry slits that dared her to argue. "You're not a good liar, Nixie. You can't pretend you don't love me."

He was right. She'd never been a good liar, partly for lack of practice, but mostly because it didn't set well with her to deceive anyone. Maybe she could hedge her way around the admission he was trying to extract from her.

She felt as though she were slapping him when, finally, after an interminable silence, she said softly, "I never told you I love you."

He looked stunned, and his grip on her hand loosened. Unwilling to witness the damage she'd inflicted on his soul, Nixie started to turn away but was stopped with a brick-hard hand on her shoulder.

When she still refused to look at him, he grasped her other shoulder and forced her to face him.

Then he kissed her with the passion of a man who saw only one chance to win back his lady's love. His determination was evident in the savage hunger of his questing lips. His hands slid from her shoulders and traveled down her sides, slowing at the slight curve of her breasts and coming to rest at the small of her back.

Nixie resisted at first, determined to deny her attraction to him. But the rightness of it, the feel of him plundering her lips—her very soul—was enough to weaken her. The muscles in the back of her knees seemed to turn to rubber, and she swayed against him. Though she hadn't thought it possible, he pulled her closer.

Under the aggressive play of his lips on her mouth, her hands relaxed from balled-up fists and slid upward around his neck.

He was far from gentle, and Nixie welcomed his roughness. His hand moved up and clutched the hair at the back of her head, preventing her retreat from the demanding possession of his ravenous kiss.

But he didn't need the force of his muscles to restrain her. She was already under his spell and had been for many years. His two-day beard rasped against her cheek, but Nixie didn't care. She wanted to envelop herself in his embrace and enjoy the warmth of his touch, the quick puffs of his breath on her skin, his overwhelming presence.

Her breathing came quick and shallow. She arched her back, exposing her neck to the wonders that his lips played upon her sensitive skin.

But just as suddenly as he had initiated the kiss, Boone released her with a shocking abruptness. Still giddy from the closeness they'd just shared, Nixie clung to him, but Boone coldly pushed her away.

Though his lips were still reddened from their pillaging forays, they were now pressed into a tight, thin line. Through the haze of her emotions, Nixie was confused at the unexpected change of attitude.

He was breathing hard, his chest rising and falling in a rhythm that tempted her to work loose the buttons on his shirt. "Now," he said through harsh breaths, "if you can tell me honestly that you don't care for me, I'll never bother you again."

Against her will, Nixie looked up into the blue eyes that dared her to deny her feelings. If she admitted the truth, she'd be choosing her own personal happiness over the well-being of her family. She had always put her family first, no matter what. And she couldn't betray them now.

Her gaze dropped from his, and she told the biggest lie of her life.

"We're not suited for each other, Boone." Taking a deep breath, she continued. "The obstacles are too big for us. Let's just forget we ever considered a serious commitment."

She couldn't bring herself to say the word "marriage," but she knew Boone understood her meaning. She could tell by his crushed look of defeat.

Ashamed of what she'd done to such a wonderful man, she turned and fled from his office.

Over the next couple of weeks, Nixie saw Boone once when she dropped off an update sheet on the donkey ball game and twice when he stopped by the house to pick up Brad for Scout meetings. The other dens weren't meeting during the summer, but Boone had reasoned the boys would welcome the chance to see their friends and get a head start on earning next year's badges.

To his credit, Boone acted toward the children as though nothing had happened between him and Nixie. She had tried to make herself scarce during his short visits, and during those times he had spent his time mumbling to Tarzan while he waited for Brad to find his Scout manual. Nixie wondered if Boone was just being friendly to the bird, or if, like Bethany, he found it easier to pour his heart out to one of God's creatures than to confide in another human.

When the day of the donkey ball game finally arrived, Boone was there early, setting out bases on the baseball diamond behind the high school. As one of the business owners who would be playing in the game, Boone wasn't required to be there early. Even though Jeff had reserved a position for him in exchange for the free advertising in his newspaper, Boone had made a pledge to the rescue squad. When business owners around the county had asked for the opportunity to play in the game, Boone had suggested Nixie put the positions up for bids. For his contribution, Boone doubled that of the top bidder.

The money would go to a good cause ... switching over to the text-enabled 911 emergency dispatch system. It was a project close to Nixie's heart, and even in such an indirect way, Boone was glad for the chance to help make her happy.

Boone returned to the ticket booth where Nixie was instructing a volunteer on the prices to charge for children and adults. Ever since he'd arrived, she had been frantically running from place to place, trying to make sure every detail was taken care of.

As she turned to rush off and flag down another volunteer, Boone caught her around the waist and pulled her to him.

Ignoring her look of surprise, he lowered his voice so the ticket taker couldn't hear. His words laden with innuendo, he whispered, "Tell me what I can do for you."

Just like old times, Boone thought as she blushed prettily. But this time, instead of wishing and wondering if she cared for him, he knew for a fact that the blush came less from embarrassment than from her own repressed desire for him.

Yes, indeed, he had solid evidence that Nixie loved him. Boone planned to press his advantage and force her to admit it. Somehow, he had to prove to her that the "obstacles" she'd cited were surmountable. He needed to prove that, between the two of them, they could leap all hurdles on their path to wedded bliss.

Just as he'd expected, she chose to take his words at face value. "You can see if the van with the donkeys has arrived yet."

"It pulled in a couple of minutes ago, and they're parking it in the outfield."

"Won't that be in the way?"

"Nah. The squishy ball they're using will keep the game near the infield."

As if suddenly aware of their proximity, she stepped back, away from the circle of his arms. Boone made no effort to stop her. She could keep physical distance from him, but he wouldn't let her push him away emotionally.

"How are Bethany and Brad?" he asked.

She lifted the damp bangs off her forehead, poked out her lower lip, and blew. "Fine. Uncle Jay and Aunt Lauren will be bringing them soon. They've been looking forward to this for a long time."

"Precious and Stormy?"

She hesitated as if suspicious of his line of questioning. "We're going to have to find Stormy a new home. I've been putting it off, hoping he and Precious would learn to get along. But now the kids have become attached to him."

Boone shoved his hands into his jeans' pockets.

"I'm sorry. If I'd known, I would have insisted on taking the kitten with me that day I found him under your bush."

"It's okay." Automatically, she touched his arm.

Yes, Boone thought, she really did care for him.

"Aunt Lauren said she and Uncle Jay would take him if it didn't work out. And the kids would still get to play with him."

Boone nodded. "And Tarzan? Has he learned any new words lately?"

Nixie smiled. Boone could tell she thought he was teasing her again with all his questions about the inhabitants of her house. She rested her hands on her back pockets, and Boone enjoyed the way the movement showed off her womanly figure.

"He hasn't learned any new words," she said, "but Bethany's been threatening to teach him to say 'Here, kitty, kitty.'"

Boone chuckled at the thought. "It would serve the bird right for all those times he made Precious jump when he barked at her." He looked at her, probing her eyes with his gaze. "And how about Nixie? Is she happy?"

Boone didn't miss how her smile faltered momentarily.

"I'm keeping busy." She looked around them at the people who were starting to arrive. "It looks like we'll have packed bleachers for the game. And I'm happy that we'll be making lots of money for the upgraded emergency dispatch system."

She hadn't said she was happy at home. Or at night when she crawled between the sheets of that big, lonely bed. Boone was glad she wasn't trying to deceive herself into believing she was happy without him.

That was half the battle won. To win the other half, Boone would have to get her to openly admit that she still loved him. And if he could win the battle, he'd have a better chance at claiming the ultimate victory ... getting her to say yes to marrying him.

❦ 13 ❧

Later, as Nixie tugged at the halter of her recalcitrant donkey, she tried not to think about the man watching her from beside his mount at first base. He was one of those deemed too large to ride the tiny animal, so the rules allowed him to run beside it or, in this case, walk and drag. Although the bleachers were packed with laughing fans, many of them calling advice to her, Nixie was unmindful of them. That one man had the power to make her feel self-conscious when all the others combined did not.

Each donkey had been trained to display a different temperament for the game. The animal's name she had drawn out of the hat had been Flash, so it had come as a surprise to discover that the little beast didn't live up to her name.

If she couldn't get the donkey to its place beyond the batter's box within the allotted amount of time,

Nixie would lose her turn at bat, earning an automatic out.

And the rescue squad and fire department couldn't afford that. The business owners had pledged to pay for every point the emergency crew scored over the opposing team. Nixie let go of the halter and walked around to the back of the animal. Giving a push, she was grateful for the donkey's mild-mannered disposition.

Gradually, with agonizing slowness, Nixie urged Flash to her appointed box. When the donkey's hoof touched the chalk line, a cheer rose up from the bleachers. Taking the rubber bat in hand, Nixie stepped up to the batter's box.

She glanced at the first baseman and squelched a giggle. The biggest man on the Bliss merchants' team, Boone had drawn the name of Tiny, the smallest donkey. Without putting weight on the animal, Boone balanced on one leg with the other draped over Tiny's back, just for show.

Winding up, the pitcher tossed the ball. Nixie made two strikes before she finally hit the padded ball with a dull thud. It rolled no more than twenty feet.

Players flew to action as they all raced for their mounts. Nixie clambered onto Flash's back and urged her toward first base. The donkey plodded along as though she were on a Sunday stroll.

Up ahead, Nixie could see the pitcher had thrown toward Boone, who missed it when Tiny came to an abrupt stop just shy of the ball. With difficulty, Boone turned his donkey with one leg while hopping with the other keep his weight off the animal—raced toward the ball. Just as Boone leaned to pick it up, Tiny knocked it with her front hoof and kicked it out of reach.

Meanwhile, Flash plodded steadily toward first base.

By now, the second baseman had figured out that his mount went left when urged right and right when steered left. By leaning in the opposite direction of where he wanted to go, he managed to work his way toward first base to back up Boone.

Nixie bounced on Flash's back, nudged her sides with the heels of her sneakers, and gently swatted her rump. No matter what she did, the animal never changed course or sped up. But it didn't matter because the other riders were just as disadvantaged as she.

Just as Flash was moseying up to the plate, Boone attempted to grab the ball and turn his miniature steed toward her. Hopping and flailing his arms, he managed to keep up with the swift-footed animal.

The pair doggedly raced toward her, and Nixie feared less that she'd score an out than that she'd get run over. When they were a few feet from her, Nixie cringed and waited for the inevitable impact.

It never came.

Boone's donkey braced her little hooves in the dirt just beyond reach of the plate and came to another bone-jarring halt. And in his enthusiasm to tag Nixie out, Boone had apparently forgotten his mount's annoying personality trait. He pitched forward from the momentum of the sudden stop and did a half flip before landing flat on his back.

In a hurry to leave the damage she'd caused, Tiny jumped over her rider and headed toward the outfield to grab a mouthful of clover.

"Boone!" Nixie had heard his audible "*Oomph!*" when he hit the ground.

Forgetting about making sure Flash's hoof touched first base, forgetting about the importance of scoring points to help earn more money for the squad, forgetting everything but the thought that Boone might be hurt as he lay motionless on the ground, Nixie jumped down and ran to him.

"Boone! Boone, are you all right?" She knelt beside him but resisted the urge to lift his head and cradle him in her arms.

From her experience running calls with the squad, she knew he could have sustained a serious injury. He may have damaged a vertebra the way he'd fallen so hard. Or he could have broken his neck or suffered a concussion.

Grabbing his wrist, she checked for a pulse. "Come on, Boone, you can't do this to me," she whispered. "Please tell me you can hear me." When he remained deathly still, Nixie felt a tear slide down her cheek. "Oh, God, Boone, I couldn't stand it if anything bad happened to you."

The other players had abandoned their donkeys, as well, and now circled them. "Is he breathing?" someone asked.

His eyes were shut, and in her panic Nixie couldn't detect whether his chest was rising and falling as it should. She laid a hand on the hard planes of his chest and leaned closer to see if she could feel his breath against her cheek.

Someone shushed the crowd, but even so, she couldn't detect any sign of respiration. She glanced at his handsome face and decided to listen again before beginning life-saving techniques. She put her ear close to his mouth.

His breath came out in a short, quick puff against her face. Startled at the unexpected response, she jerked around and looked into his smiling eyes.

"Go ahead and admit it, Nixie. You *do* love me."

He had set her up. And Nixie had fallen for it like a row of dominoes.

It was Saturday morning, the day after Boone's hoax, yet she still couldn't stop thinking about the scare he'd given her. And the awkward part was that, with all those people crowded around them, she couldn't deny what he'd said.

All she could do was drown him with her tears of relief and promise him that if he ever pulled another stunt like that, she'd personally give him a concussion.

Jeff finished backing the ambulance into the squad building's bay. Nixie got out and pressed the button to lower the automatic door. Thanks to it being a weekend, they'd managed to pick up a third volunteer, Marvin, who had helped considerably on the rescue call.

"I'm glad old Mr. Binford is going to be all right," Marvin said. "The way he was breathing, he had me pretty worried."

Nixie chuckled as she recalled their trip to the emergency room with the elderly man gasping for breath. It wasn't until Marvin had started questioning the man's daughter that they discovered the reason for his breathing problem. At age eighty-nine, Mr. Binford was unable to get around as much as he used to, so his daughter had installed a deluxe cable television service for him to watch. The old man had clicked through the channels until he found a program featuring women wrestlers. After a few moments of viewing, he had hyperventilated.

"I wish all our calls were this easy. Fix the problem, then cart 'em to the hospital to be checked out." Nixie snapped her fingers. "Just like that."

A few minutes later, as she pulled into her driveway, Nixie decided she'd have to tell Uncle Jay what happened to Bo Binford. She checked the mailbox and found one envelope. The return address was that of the *Bliss Gazette*. Something from Boone?

With tentative fingers, she opened the letter. It was from Aunt Alice, the advice columnist. Nixie had almost forgotten she'd sent that letter in which she'd poured out her frustrations. Too late, she realized the embarrassment she could have caused if the letter had been used in the newspaper column. Thank goodness Aunt Alice had chosen to reply personally.

Dear Reader,

It appears your daughter did, indeed, want a father, but perhaps she expected a generic man who could be a companion to her mother and a helper to her and her brother. From what you told me in your letter, it seems she didn't expect to involve her heart any more than if she were hiring a gardener. Yet, things turned out differently than she expected, and she began to love this man who recently re-entered your life. Have you considered that she may feel disloyal to her deceased father by loving another man?

Nixie stared at the letter in amazement. She had been trying for weeks to figure out what was bothering Bethany, and the only thing she could conclude was that her daughter was just as confused by her reaction to Boone as she was. And yet an advice columnist—a complete stranger—was able to sum up the problem in a mere paragraph. Nixie couldn't help being astonished by the writer's perception and insight.

The letter concluded:

Remember that children don't always know what's best for them. Be honest with the man you love and tell him what you told me. With the help of his love and understand-

ing, both of you can help your daughter cope with her ambiguous feelings.

For the next several days, Nixie's thoughts kept returning to Alice's letter. Why hadn't she seen that Bethany's resistance reflected her loyalty to her father's memory? Nixie supposed she had overlooked that possibility because Bethany had been so young when Paul died.

One thing was certain. Bethany had been receptive to Boone and enjoyed his friendship until they'd begun talking about marriage.

If her daughter had truly disliked him, Nixie's decision to break things off with Boone would have been a little easier to bear. But she knew that Bethany cared for him as much as Brad did. That was what made things so frustrating.

🦋 14 🦋

Her heart ached as she thought of the pain she'd put Boone through. But, she reminded herself, she hadn't known what else to do at the time.

Nixie walked into the living room and noticed that Brad had forgotten to cover Tarzan before he went to bed. Pulling the cloth up over the bird's cage, she whispered, "Night-night."

"Night-night," the parrot echoed. Then the bird whispered a phrase she'd never heard him say before. In fact, she'd never heard the loudmouth whisper until now.

She listened closely, waiting for him to repeat the phrase. When he did, she couldn't believe her ears.

"Boone loves Nixie," the bird confided in a hushed croak.

Shocked, Nixie echoed the statement as if to verify what she'd just heard. "Boone loves Nixie?"

Tarzan sidestepped closer on his perch and peered at her through the bars with one beady eye. "Boone loves Nixie," he whispered several times in succession. Then he shocked her back to reality by shrieking, *"Ha-ha-ha-ha-ha-ha-ha-ha."* Stunned, Nixie finished covering the cage.

"Night-night," Tarzan peeped. Then he began quietly practicing the new sentence he'd just mastered.

Her mind still reeling, she stumbled into the kitchen to catch Stormy and lock him up for the night. Warm with emotion from the bird's whispered revelation, Nixie hugged the little brown kitten.

"Boone loves Nixie," she said to the squirming animal. "That must have been what he was mumbling to Tarzan all those times I found him by the cage."

The advice columnist's suggestion came back to her. *Be honest with the man you love.* Although she loved Boone with all her heart, she'd never told him—not even after his tumble at the donkey ball game. He would be coming tomorrow to take Brad to the den meeting. She'd tell him then. She'd also enlist his aid in helping Bethany cope with her "ambiguous feelings."

For the first time in a long while, Nixie's spirits soared. There was hope, after all. And that hope empowered her, made her sense that, together, she and Boone could accomplish anything. That they could even make Bethany realize there was room in their family, and in her heart, for a newcomer such as Boone.

Precious rubbed against her legs, demanding a bedtime snack, so she put Stormy down on the floor, reached into the pantry, and retrieved a can of the cat's favorite flavor. Chicken chunks in sauce. She opened the can and turned to get their bowls. Precious stood in front of Stormy with her back arched and fur standing on end. The yellow cat bared her teeth and hissed at the newcomer.

"Stop that," Nixie said and stamped her foot at Precious. Remembering the overheard conversation Bethany had with her cat, she wished there was a way to get the animals to become friends. Maybe if her daughter saw that Precious could accept an animal newcomer, then Bethany could accept a human one.

As she scooped the smelly stuff into the cat's dish, an idea occurred to Nixie. It was a far-fetched idea, but at this point Nixie was willing to try anything.

Ignoring the angry hisses from Precious, she picked up the lanky kitten and cuddled him close. "Please excuse what I'm about to do to you," she told the brown feline. "But if this works, we'll both be thanking each other."

That said, Nixie plunged her fingertips into the gravy-like sauce. Cooing all the while to the bewildered kitten, she stroked its head and left a patch of sauce smeared on its fur.

"On the other hand, if this doesn't work," she told

him, "I'll have to give you the added indignity of a bath."

A few more strokes, and Stormy was covered with cat food sauce from his eyebrows to his ear tips and down his neck. "Please let this work," Nixie murmured and set him on the floor near Precious.

The older cat hissed again. But just as she'd hoped, Precious suddenly stopped complaining and leaned forward, sniffing suspiciously. Moving closer, the cat sniffed her tiny counterpart.

Anxious, Nixie stood ready to intervene if the old-timer should attack the kitten.

Slowly, tentatively, Precious stretched until her mouth was at Stormy's neck. Nixie prayed fervently that Precious wouldn't do to the kitten what she had done to the chipmunk she'd caught last month.

When the yellow cat's tongue darted out to sample the aromatic kitten, Nixie breathed a sigh of relief. Soon Precious was happily cleaning the sauce off of Stormy's head, and Stormy was obviously enjoying the older cat's rough massage. But after the sauce was gone, instinct took over, and Precious gave Stormy a thorough washing.

Nixie put her hands together, looked heavenward, and whispered a heartfelt "Thank you."

Later, after she'd dressed for bed, she went looking for Stormy, hoping she wouldn't have to lock him in the utility room again. After a thorough inspection of the house, she finally found him in Bethany's room, snuggled on the ragged blanket that served as a bed for Precious. The older cat's yellow paw lay draped across the tiny kitten as they slept.

Nixie closed the door and went back to her bedroom. If only it could be this simple for Boone to win Bethany's acceptance.

Wednesday evening, when Boone stopped by to pick up Brad for the Scout meeting, Nixie was ready for him.

Instead of pulling her hair back with clips as she often did to keep it out of the way, she'd spent a long time at the bathroom mirror, puffing her bangs and coaxing the reddish-brown locks into gentle waves that caressed her shoulders.

Even at her age, when she was old enough to know it didn't matter about the size of her endowments, she wished she had a little more on top. But she did have good legs, so she pulled on a pair of black stretch pants that would show them to their best advantage and topped everything off with an oversize red shirt that fell below her hips.

Nixie had a lot to make up to Boone, and she wanted to give him every reason possible to forgive her for her foolish mistake. She only hoped it wasn't too late.

He prowled the den, waiting once again for Brad to gather his belongings so they could go. Nixie was pleased that even though Boone seemed restless, he wasn't too distracted to notice the fit of her clothes. He gave her a once-over that would have earned any other man a slap for his familiarity. Coming from Boone, though, the intense observation made her feel twenty years old again. Young, vibrant, and alluring.

Nixie mentally reviewed her game plan, just as Boone had always done before going out on the football field. Remembering Aunt Alice's suggestion to be honest with the man she loved, she would begin by telling him her feelings for him. She'd follow by saying that, if he was still willing, she would welcome his presence—and especially his love and under-standing—through the good times and bad in her life. And she'd be there for him through the good and bad times in his life.

She would have to warn him, though, that they needed to take things slowly with Bethany. But, in doing so, that would give them time to learn more about each other and solidify their relationship before taking that giant step into marriage.

Boone's nervous prowling took him past Tarzan's cage. He paused and grinned at the bird. "Has he learned anything new recently?" he asked Nixie.

This was the opening she'd been waiting for. But first, she'd dish out a little of the teasing he'd given her so much of over the years. "Besides burping and excusing himself?"

Brad burst into the room with the subtlety of a train wreck. "I'm ready, Boone, let's go."

Boone caught the boy by the scruff of his shirt. "Wait a minute. What's your hurry?"

"He wants to get there first," Bethany said, descending the stairs with ladylike poise, "because he wants to sit next to you."

"I can't blame him for that," Nixie said. An eyebrow raised, Boone turned and cast her a curious glance. Nixie met his gaze with a slight fluttering of her eyelashes. She hoped she wasn't overdoing it. Although he seemed encouraged by her response, she couldn't open the door to the discussion she'd planned—not with the children in the room.

"I have a surprise for all of you," Boone announced, reaching into his back pocket.

Brad crowded closer to his idol while Bethany pretended little interest in the papers in his hand.

"Three more applicants," Boone said, holding the papers aloft.

Brad followed him to the sofa and sat down beside him, a frown creasing his youthful features. "I don't want a stranger for a daddy. I want you."

Boone squeezed the boy's shoulder. Together, Nixie and Boone turned to Bethany for her reaction.

The girl sat down beside her brother. Her expression was troubled, and Nixie couldn't help worrying that her daughter's discomfort might erupt in a physical form as it had done before.

"I'd like to see the replies," Bethany told Boone.

Nixie's heart sank. When the preteen had awakened this morning to find Stormy and Precious playing together like the best of buddies, she had been ecstatic.

When Nixie had entered the room to find Bethany playing with both cats, she had tried to point out to her daughter that Precious could accept Stormy and still love her. Nixie tried to make her realize, without coming right out and saying so, that Bethany could accept Boone into her life and still love Paul.

Apparently, the message hadn't sunk in.

Boone handed Bethany the three pieces of correspondence. Two emails and one snail-mail letter. "I didn't think you'd get any more responses since the ad stopped running a long time ago," he told her. "These folks must have found an old newspaper lying around, or they might have planned to answer the ad but took a long time getting around to it."

Bethany scanned the first email while the three of them watched. After a moment she crumpled it into a ball, as she'd done with so many of the others.

"This loser thinks it's okay to use drugs for 'recreational purposes,'" she said with a sneer in her voice.

Despite her disappointment that Bethany was still unwilling to give Boone a chance, Nixie smiled her relief. Apparently the *Too Smart to Start* message was firmly embedded in her daughter's attitude.

"How about the next one?" Boone asked.

Nixie blinked and glared at him with sharp disapproval. Why was he encouraging her? With a heavy sigh, she realized she couldn't blame him. After all, she'd been the one to tell him in no uncertain terms that there was no chance of a permanent relationship between them.

Bethany unfolded the second email in the stack. "This one's a farmer."

Apparently forgetting his earlier declaration about wanting only Boone for a daddy, Brad perked up and peered over his sister's shoulder. "Hey, maybe we could learn how to milk a cow!"

"Not this one," Bethany said, tearing it in two. "He just wants us for extra help on the farm. *I'm* not going to ballet lessons smelling like cow dookie."

"Too late," Brad razzed. "You already do."

Nixie sought to soften the disappointment that was evident in her daughter's face. "Bethany, this is why I was against your placing the ad for a daddy. It's hard enough to find a decent single man, and an ad such as yours and Brad's seems to bring responses from people who are most desperate."

Bethany scowled. "But I've heard about how people met through dating apps and classified ads."

Nixie felt her daughter's pain. Sitting beside her, she put an arm around the child. "Those stories make the news because successes are so rare."

"Well, don't give up yet," Boone urged. "There's one more in your hand."

Nixie tried not to feel the pain that his words caused. He seemed too willing to find a replacement.

Bethany's pessimism was obvious as she slowly opened the last one, but her eyes widened as she pulled the letter from its envelope. "This one's typed."

"It's a long one, too," Brad piped in. "Read it out loud."

Bethany cleared her throat and began.

Dear Children,

I am impressed by your enterprise, as well as your obvious high opinion of your mother. I trust she realizes how lucky she is to have thoughtful children such as yourselves.

Bethany stopped and scratched her nose. "So far, so good. He must have good taste to recognize how wonderful we are." She smiled and continued.

Since beauty is in the eye of the beholder, I won't bother to describe my physical attributes. Why don't we let your mother decide for herself whether I meet her standards?

As for the other points you specified in your ad, I confess I strive to be strong in character as well as in physical fitness. I was raised in a loving home, and I look forward to sharing my love with a woman who wants to be my equal yet is willing to accept that the differences in men and women serve to complement the whole.

Though I don't currently share my home with any animals, I am fond of all of God's creatures, especially children.

"God's creatures," Brad said. "He sounds like a churchgoer." He licked his finger and stroked the air. "That's another point for him."

You asked for someone who is dependable. I trust that you'll accept my ownership of a prominent business in your community as evidence that I am up to handling my respon-

sibilities. Because of my professional endeavors, I must ask your understanding about my choosing to remain anonymous until your mother decides whether she'd like to meet me.

The letter ended with a suggestion they meet at seven o'clock Saturday night at an elegant restaurant just outside of town. Nixie would be able to identify the mystery man by the red carnation on his lapel.

"That's an expensive restaurant," Bethany observed. "I wonder if he's rich."

"He used a bunch of big words," said Brad. "I'll bet he's plenty smart enough for Mom."

Boone leaned forward and looked past the children to catch Nixie's eye. "This one sounds like a winner. Why don't you meet him?"

"Yeah," said Bethany. "It couldn't hurt."

Brad, on the other hand, got up and jerked his Scout manual off the lamp table. "It sounds like a stupid idea to me." Turning to Boone, he added, "Let's go, or we're going to be late."

Boone rose slowly, passing Nixie a wink as he did so. "Where's your sense of adventure, boy? I think it would be a good idea for your mother to meet this Mr. Wonderful."

Nixie rose and followed them to the door. "Boone, I don't think that's a good idea."

"Hey, it's a great idea. If you're scared of meeting a stranger, I'll go and sit at another table to keep an eye on things."

"That won't be necessary, because I'm not going."

"What do you mean, you're not going? This guy has winner written all over him."

Nixie took a deep breath. Maybe she should go ahead and tell him now, in front of the children. Let him know she wasn't a lost cause where he was concerned. Silently, she willed him to understand what she was trying so hard to communicate to him.

"There's something important I have to tell you."

"We're going to be late. Let's talk when we get back. Meanwhile, mark your calendar for Saturday night. I want you to give this guy a try."

Nixie's throat closed at the cavalier manner in which he urged her to see another man. All she could manage to force out was one word. "Why?"

Boone stepped out onto the porch. Holding the screen door open, he gave a little shrug. "I want you and the kids to be happy."

❧ 15 ❧

Nixie stepped into the shimmery black dress, then turned around for Aunt Lauren to zip it up.

"I ought to have my head examined," she told her aunt, "for agreeing to go out with a complete stranger." Aunt Lauren connected the hook and eye at the top of the dress and patted Nixie's back. "The mystery man sounds like quite a catch. Don't you think he's intriguing?"

Nixie nodded. He did, indeed, sound intriguing. Under other circumstances, she would have been more enthusiastic about meeting the man who'd sent that endearing letter. But her heart already belonged to Boone, and any other man paled by comparison.

She had been prepared to open her heart to Boone and let him know how much she cared for him. But by the time he'd brought Brad home from the Scout meeting, he had convinced her son that it was in her best interest to meet the man. Neither gave her an opportunity to say what was on her mind —and in her heart. And soon Bethany was urging her to meet "Mr. Wonderful."

Nixie had cried herself to sleep that night. It hurt to know that the man she loved was trying so hard to get rid of her. He had obviously changed his mind about wanting to marry her, and though she considered begging him for another chance, she couldn't bring herself to do it.

She shaded her eyes as Aunt Lauren tucked a stray bit of hair into the elaborate braid and sprayed it into place.

"I won't be out late," Nixie said. "Please don't let Uncle Jay give the children too much junk food while I'm gone."

"Don't you worry about us. You just go and have a good time."

A good time. She doubted it. Nixie hoped Mr. Wonderful would be able to forgive her for ruining *his* evening. She was certain she wouldn't be very good company tonight. How could she, when she would spend the whole evening thinking about Boone?

"Park in a lighted area," Uncle Jay told her as she was leaving the house. "And ask the *maître d'* for a table that's out in the open where you can be seen by the other diners. Just in case he gets fresh, you know."

With a grin, Nixie pointed to her narrow-toed

black shoes. "Don't worry. These should be a good deterrent."

∼

Nixie arrived too early at the restaurant. First, she'd overestimated how long it would take to get there. Then, in their eagerness, her family had whisked her out the door fifteen minutes sooner than she'd planned to leave.

Remembering her uncle's advice, she requested a table near the center of the restaurant. The waiter brought her a glass of white wine. She sipped it, hoping Mr. Wonderful would arrive soon so they could hurry and get this over with.

She was studying the wallpaper pattern when a flurry of activity caught her attention as a small group descended upon a nearby table. The boy caught her attention first. His blond hair was slicked back, and the kid sported a clip-on tie, white shirt, and jeans.

Brad turned in his seat, grinned at Nixie, and waggled his fingers in a friendly wave.

Brad! What was he doing here? And Bethany. And Uncle Jay and Aunt Lauren! The whole family had turned out to gawk at her mysterious stranger.

Nixie got up and walked over to their table. "Get a sudden craving for escargot?" she asked. "Or did you run out of videos and need something else to watch?"

Everyone started talking at once, making excuses

for their unexpected appearance. It was obvious they had planned to come all along. How else could they have changed their clothes and arrived at the restaurant so soon after she did? Nixie gave them a beleaguered look.

Bethany spoke up. "We'll be as quiet as mice. Just pretend you don't know us."

Uncle Jay and Aunt Lauren murmured their agreement. Nixie met Aunt Lauren's eyes. "It doesn't surprise me that Uncle Jay would show up here. But *you?*"

Aunt Lauren gave her a guilty smile. "I couldn't help it, dear. I was just dying of curiosity."

After Aunt Lauren assured her there would be no audible comments from the table and that they'd try not to stare, Nixie went back to her seat.

She took another sip of the wine and checked her watch. Six fifty-five. Her pulse was racing. Why was she so nervous about someone she didn't even want to meet? Nixie supposed it had something to do with the dread that settled over her. She felt guilty for wasting the man's time, not to mention his money, when she wasn't a bit interested in him. Checking her purse for a credit card, she decided the least she could do was pay for her own meal.

Someone appeared beside her with an armful of flowers. Nervous, Nixie stood and almost knocked over her chair. "Glad to meet—" In a split second she took in the dark, well-cut suit before her gaze traveled up to his face.

"Boone! You, too?"

She took the flowers he offered her. Although she was touched by his show of support, she was beginning to feel like a circus sideshow.

"The flowers are a nice touch," she said. Glancing around the restaurant, she noticed a man who had just come in. Maybe that was Mr. Wonderful. The last thing she wanted to do was embarrass him with Boone's presence. "Look, maybe you should go now."

He grinned but made no move to leave. Then Nixie noticed it.

The bright splash of red on his lapel.

As realization dawned on her, Nixie returned his grin. Boone was the mystery man.

Mr. Wonderful. His qualifications were perfect. Her aunt and uncle said so. Brad said so. Even Bethany had agreed that this latest candidate sounded like the perfect match for Nixie.

Nixie was pleased with this turn of events and knew it would thrill the rest of her family, but what about Bethany?

Taking the bouquet from Nixie, Boone laid it on the table, then assisted with her chair as she took her seat. Nixie couldn't help experiencing a sudden giddiness that she knew was unrelated to the few sips of wine she'd had before he arrived.

Boone sat across from her and reached for her hand.

Nixie clasped his big fingers. "There's something I wanted to tell you last Wednesday."

"There will be plenty of time for that," Boone interrupted. "But first, I have a couple of confessions to make."

Nixie's heart sank. Was he getting ready to play another joke on her?

"As you've probably already guessed, I'm the guy who wrote that last letter." With his free hand, he loosened the knot in his tie. "The other letters, though, were sort of ... uh, invented."

Nixie's thoughts tumbled through her brain. "You wrote them?" At his affirmative nod, she lost it. "Why would you do something like that? How dare you toy with my children's emotions!"

She tried to withdraw her hand from his grasp, but he held tight.

"Please. I wasn't trying to hurt your kids. I love them too much to do that." He took a sip of water, and it seemed as though he had a hard time swallowing. "I didn't want them to be disappointed when they didn't get any responses to their ad. Besides, it seemed like a good excuse for me to come and see you and the kids."

"So, they were all fake."

Boone gave her a sheepish grin. "All but the one from the felon."

The waiter arrived, delaying their conversation for a moment. Nixie was glad for the interruption since it gave her time to collect her emotions.

Although she thought it was unwise for him to string them along as he had, she was convinced his intentions were pure. And truthfully, she was glad things worked out the way they had.

After the waiter left with their orders, Boone made another startling revelation. "While I'm coming clean, I might as well tell you I'm Aunt Alice."

Nixie felt the blood drain from her face. "Oh, my gosh."

"I wish you had told me why you turned me down."

"If you knew, why didn't you say something?"

Boone looked down at his tie clip and fiddled with it before answering. "I figured you needed some space." Looking up, he added, "I still want you to marry me."

He was giving her another chance. And she wasn't going to let it slip through her fingers again. "A very wise person once told me I should be honest with the man I love ... and I do love you, Boone."

"Will you marry me?"

She answered without hesitation. "Yes."

"What about Bethany? If she's still having a problem with us getting married, I don't want to cause another outbreak of hives."

Nixie had forgotten all about Bethany's objections. Remembering Aunt Alice's sage advice, she acknowledged that children don't always know what's best for them. Somehow, she'd have to convince her daughter that Boone would be a wonderful addition to the family.

"My answer will still be yes," she said, "but I want it to be with my family's blessing."

Excusing herself, Nixie went to the table where her family was eagerly observing their interchange. Uncle Jay pulled up a chair for her.

"Boone has asked me to marry him, and I want to tell him yes," she told her loved ones. Brad cheered, and Aunt Lauren and Uncle Jay smiled at each other. "But not if it means causing divisiveness between me and my children."

Bethany ducked her head and grabbed for a napkin to wipe her eyes.

"I think Bethany and I need to go to the powder room," she told her family. "We'll be right back."

In the privacy of the restroom lounge, Nixie spoke firmly with her daughter. Praying that Bethany wouldn't have another outbreak of nerves, she told her how much she loved Boone. "Even you agreed he was the perfect candidate to be your dad. Don't you like Boone?"

Bethany sobbed again, and Nixie handed her a fresh tissue.

"I do like Boone, and I want him in the family, but—"

"But what?"

"I don't want to hurt Uncle Jay's feelings."

Because she and her daughter were close, Nixie thought she'd understood Bethany's reluctance to accept Boone. But her announcement shattered

Nixie's assumption that Bethany was merely being loyal to her father. *"Uncle Jay?"*

Bethany nodded. "He always calls me his favorite little girl."

Nixie groaned. All along, Bethany had been afraid of being disloyal to her uncle. She sat beside her daughter on the plush burgundy carousel. Maybe she could still make the cat analogy work. "Did you stop loving Precious when Stormy came along?"

"Of course not."

"Do you love Stormy more than you love Precious?"

"No. They're so different that it's hard to compare. I love Stormy because he's playful and funny, but I love Precious because she's sweet, and she makes me feel better when I'm sad."

"Is Precious jealous when you play with Stormy?"

Bethany threw her a suspicious look. "Not since they became friends." Suddenly, she became enthusiastic. "You know, it's even more fun playing with both cats than just one at a time."

Nixie smiled. At last there was hope.

"Hey," said Bethany. "Do you think it would be the same with Uncle Jay and Boone?"

Breakthrough! She tried to control her exhilaration as she and Bethany walked back to the table. "Uncle Jay was willing to share you with Brad when your little brother came along. I'm sure he wouldn't mind sharing you with Boone."

Bethany gave her an impulsive hug.

Nixie walked back to Boone and gave him a thumbs-up. She thought he was going to help her with her chair again, but instead, he guided her back to her family's table and urged her to join them.

Then he dropped to one knee. His eyes were on Nixie, but his words addressed them all. "Will y'all marry me?"

The answer was a chorus of five yeses.

The tears that flowed from Nixie's eyes were tears of happiness. It had taken them fifteen years to realize they had loved each other all along. And now the people dearest to her agreed they belonged together. Nixie didn't think she'd ever been happier in her entire life.

Boone stood and urged her into his arms, the best place in the world for her to be.

Standing there, tears leaking onto his shirt, Nixie was aware that all eyes in the restaurant were upon them. But she didn't care. All that mattered was that she and Boone and her family were going to be together at last.

"It's unanimous," she whispered. "We'll marry you."

Dear Reader,

Readers are an author's life blood and the stories couldn't happen without you. Thank you so much for reading. If you enjoyed *Boone,* we would so appreciate a review. You have no idea how much it means to us!

To read an excerpt of the next book in Sweet Southern Charmers series, *Colton,* please turn the page.

If you'd like to keep up with latest releases, you can sign up for my newsletter @ https://loriwilde.com/subscribe/

To check out other books, you can visit Lori on the web @ www.loriwilde.com.

Much love and light!

—Lori & Carolyn

EXCERPT: COLTON

"Give it to me, sweetie. Don't make me fight you for it." April Hanson crouched lower with her hand outstretched to the beautiful but goofy golden retriever.

Unfortunately, Maybelline had decided that a game of tag was in order. This happened every time she tried to teach the dog to fetch—only this time it was no newspaper they were battling over. The dog darted to one side, its rump stuck playfully in the air and a small gray object hanging from its mouth.

Straightening, April ran a hand through the blonde bangs that tickled her forehead. The direct approach obviously wouldn't work. But maybe she could distract Maybelline before the dog accidentally injured the baby squirrel she'd found.

Assuming a nonchalance she didn't feel, she strolled over to the base of the tree where the remains of the nest lay scattered on the ground. April guessed it had been ransacked by a hawk or an opossum.

She bent and picked up a burl from the ground. Maybelline's ears pricked forward in curiosity, and April teased the dog with the gnarled wood, holding it first behind her back, and then swinging it from side to side, just out of Maybelline's reach.

Just as she'd hoped, the retriever couldn't resist. When the small gray bundle dropped, forgotten, from the dog's mouth, April hurled the bit of wood as hard as she could into the thicket and made a move to run after it herself.

Sure enough, Maybelline rose to the challenge and went dashing off after it.

April gently picked up the young squirrel. Fortunately, it seemed unharmed by not only the nest marauder but Maybelline's teeth, as well. She cradled the squirrel to her chest in an attempt to warm it. The poor creature's eyes were not yet open, leading April to guess it was only about three or four weeks old.

"Poor sweet baby," she cooed. "You really got off to a rocky start, didn't you?"

Running a finger lightly over the tiny body, April hoped the squirrel hadn't been too stressed by the recent events in its short life. When it curled into a ball, April tucked the sleepy foundling down between her T-shirt and outer shirt. It squirmed until it found a comfy spot at her waist, then settled down for a nap. She would have to get little Rocky home soon and find him some milk.

April remounted her horse and placed a protective hand around the makeshift baby carrier. This was so typical of the way things turned out for her.

She'd been wanting a baby of her own and look at what she ended up with. If that was how God answered prayers, then she supposed He must have a really whacked sense of humor.

On the ride back to the campground office, April quickly finished her inspection, making note of fallen trees that needed to be cleared, as well as a blockage in the swollen stream that meandered its way to the man-made lake below.

Maybelline nosed in a pile of leaves, found a dried pinecone, and dashed away with the prize in her mouth. April touched her heels to the horse's ribs. The horse paused to nibble from a low-hanging branch.

"Come on, Daisy, let's go back to the stable and get some hay instead of those yucky dead leaves."

It was a beautiful spring morning. The Virginia weather had grown warm enough for shirtsleeves, and the trees had started budding, some of which burst forth with bright-green leaves.

The small bay mare, unable to contain her pent-up energy, stamped her hoof when April refused to loosen the reins for a gallop back to the stable.

When they neared the camp store, she noticed that

the crocus bulbs she'd planted last fall had sprung up several inches in just a few days. A robin landed among the new shoots, snagged a blade of dry grass, and carried it off in its beak, presumably to line its nest.

"Good grief, it looks like the whole world is full of birth and new life."

Daisy's ears swiveled back at the brittle tone in her rider's voice.

"What are you looking so innocent for?" April asked. "I haven't forgotten how you decided to go gallivanting through the countryside, looking for a date. Old Man Grissom hasn't been the same since you stood outside his paddock, batting your eyelashes at his prize jumper stallion until Majesty's Thunder came over the fence after you."

The mare shook her mane, making it seem as though she was disagreeing with what April said.

"Knowing my luck, you're probably in foal and I'll have to pay a huge stud fee." Begrudgingly, she added, "At least you know how to pick 'em."

Unlike me, she added mentally and rubbed the tiny bundle at her waist. If she'd known how to pick a mate, she'd be married and have a houseful of snotty-nosed kids by now. April sighed.

What she wouldn't give to have a half dozen little noses, mouths, hands, and butts to wipe. Instead, at thirty-six, the sound of her biological clock was no longer just ticking but clanging away like crazy.

She loved the children she worked with as camp activity director, but April didn't know if she'd be able to take another season of watching parents flaunting their children. She knew they didn't actually *flaunt* them, but her long-unfulfilled desire to have a baby of her own made their teasing comments feel like a physical punch—right in the womb. "You want kids? Take mine." If only those people knew how much she wanted to take them up on their joking offers.

She rode up to the hitching post in front of the camp store, and her business partner stepped out onto the board planks.

Colton Radway stood there, looking at her ... *expectantly*.

Of course.

"What's the matter?" she asked.

"How about dinner and a movie tonight?" he suggested as he had every day for the past couple of years.

And just as she had done every day he asked that question, she ignored it. "No, really, what's wrong?"

"Nothing's wrong. Your niece called."

"Nicole? What did she want?"

Colton, her lifelong best friend and the man whom only she referred to as "Buddy," rocked back on his heels and rubbed the tension from his eyebrows. She'd seen that gesture a million times before, and *usually* it meant trouble.

"She didn't *want* anything. She has something to tell you." He reached into his back pocket and pulled out a cell phone.

"Oh, my gosh, something's wrong. I know it is."

He handed her the phone. "So, call her then."

"No."

She swung her leg over Daisy's neck. As she jumped down, Colton caught her waist, then cast a curious eye at the movement under her shirt.

"Squirrel," she said in explanation.

Obviously accustomed by now to the many orphaned creatures she brought back with her to mother, he didn't question further. He waited for her to take the cell phone.

Standing in front of him, closer now but still well below his eye level, April pushed the phone away. "The last two times Nicole called with something to tell me, she'd either eloped with that computer geek or been involved in a car accident."

Family members often said Nicole was enough like April to be her clone. So, it was no wonder that whenever her twenty-two-year-old niece got into trouble, she called her aunt to help her out of it.

"You know how I am with bad news," April told Colton. "Just tell me what she said so I can prepare for the worst."

Exasperated, Colton blurted, "You're going to be a great aunt. Okay?"

At April's strangled gasp, Daisy turned to look at her. April could have sworn the horse smiled.

Great aunt! She was too young to be a great aunt. Great aunts were always old, with gnarled, arthritic hands and thick bifocals. Just last year, April had to get glasses for the first time after she started having difficulty reading small print.

She looked down at her hands and studied the sprinkling of brown dots that she'd seen a million times and only just now really noticed. She'd always assumed they were freckles. But what if they were liver spots?

"Is something the matter?" Colton asked.

Of course, something was the matter. Her niece was pregnant, and *she* wasn't!

Colton pushed his ever-present Western hat back from his forehead and rubbed his eyebrows.

"I'm only thirty-six."

"True, but Nicole is a grown woman. Besides, she's married, so there's no reason to get upset."

The comment was a veiled reference to her mother's reaction to her sister's senior-year announcement that she was pregnant. The elder Hanson had reacted poorly to Stella's having a baby out of wedlock. Things hadn't changed much since then. Most of the folks in the small town of Bliss had similar traditional thoughts, and heaven help the person who failed to abide by their expectations.

"Yes, thank goodness she's married," April agreed. "Looks like Nicole managed to get John's mind off his computer—at least once."

Colton studied her for a moment, a concerned frown marring the handsome lines of his face. Then he put an arm around her shoulders. "He's not a bad guy, you know."

He was right. Perhaps her problem with John was jealousy. Nicole had someone with whom to start a family. And she didn't.

"Yeah, I suppose he'll be a good father." She looked up at Colton and smiled. "He'd *better* be a good father."

Colton smiled and handed her the phone. "Call Nicole. She can't wait to tell you the good news." He took Daisy's reins and turned to lead her back to the stable. Speaking over his shoulder, he added, "And try to sound like it's the first time you heard it."

April held the phone in her liver-spotted hands. Without her glasses, the numbers on the keypad were slightly blurred from this distance. She held the appliance at arm's length and squinted. There, that was better.

A sudden sense of panic came over April. If she was ever going to have a baby, she needed to do it now. If she waited any longer, she'd have gray hair by the time her child was ready to enroll in kindergarten.

This was ridiculous. First, she spent a couple of years married to the wrong man. Then she spent several more years looking for the right man who, by the way, never showed up. After that, she devoted most of her energy to working with Colton to turn the campground into a profit maker.

As the years slowly slipped away, so did her opportunities for finding a good husband and father. Most of the men in her age range were either firmly married or entering their midlife crises and looking for women at least ten years younger than April. With each passing year, the slim pickings became even more meager.

A growing plume of dust in the distance caught her attention. Down the graveled road that led into the campground, a small dot of a car approached. Probably a family coming for an early-in-the-season weekend camping trip. She hoped they didn't have a baby or toddler with them.

The coming summer months would only bring more babies, toddlers, and elementary school-age children to their campground, and she would be responsible for keeping them entertained with age-appropriate activities. She knew she couldn't take another season of coveting other people's children.

She closed the cover on the phone. She would call her niece after she got this family settled into a campsite. And even if she had to grit her teeth while doing it, she would sound happy for Nicole.

Watching the dust plume come closer, April felt her spirits lift as soon as she settled upon a course of action. *There's no time like the present,* Colton always said.

Little Rocky wiggled at her waist as if to reinforce the thought that had entered her head.

She was going to have a baby no matter what it took. A smile formed on her lips, and relief settled over her heart at the decision she'd made. Making up her mind was the easy part. The true test of character would be following through with the plan.

The car pulled into the parking lot, but this was no family to torment her with a car full of adorable children. It was one of the sheriff's department vehicles.

The deputy got out, stretched, and took a leisurely look around.

"The camping season has hardly started," April said. "Surely Mrs. Turner doesn't have anything to complain about already."

The man closed the car door and pocketed the key. Stepping forward with a swagger that seemed forced on someone of his short stature, he hooked his thumbs through his belt loops and smiled. The weekend deputy's name badge, obviously carefully polished, winked at her in the sunlight. Dugg, it read. She'd heard he was a salesclerk at Reece Masardi's feed and seed store Monday through Friday. His part-time job, however, was what he lived for.

"It's not your campers that's bothering Mrs. Turner this time," he drawled. "I understand you have a young hoodlum working for you now."

"Steven is a kid who's trying to turn his life around. I won't have anyone, including you, referring to him in that manner."

As he drew himself up and squared his shoulders, April could tell she'd made a mistake. Despite his effort at appearing more authoritative, her riding boots gave her an inch on him in height. That and her statement served to undermine the tenuous hold he had on the respect he seemed to crave. But right now, April didn't care about his personal agenda. She was more concerned about Steven.

Dugg had been a repeat visitor to their campground ever since the elderly Bea Turner had moved into the house at the near corner of the campground last summer. He seemed to relish the "showdown" between the two neighbors and gleefully issued repeated warnings and citations. A couple of times she and Colton had had to appear in court for disturbing the peace, all because of the dance contests she staged for the teenagers each Friday night during their busy season. The music was always silenced by eleven o'clock, but that never stopped the determined deputy from writing up yet another darned citation.

The woman had not stopped complaining since she'd moved in. There had been letters to the editor of the local newspaper, griping to other residents, and even an attempt to raise a petition against the campground's "noisy activities."

Fortunately, no one other than Mrs. Turner had a complaint against them. But she was still managing to make life difficult for them.

Since most of their activities took place on the weekends, they'd come to know the over enthusiastic Alexander Dugg better than they would have liked.

Colton returned from the barn and stood beside April in a show of solidarity. The twitching muscle in his jaw was his only outward sign of annoyance. His voice came out in a deep rumble. "Is there a problem, Deputy Dugg?"

April almost smiled as her partner slurred the last two words until they sounded like the name of an old-time cartoon dog. There was no mistaking he'd done it intentionally.

"It seems as though that reform school dropout of yours was loitering behind your neighbor's shed yesterday. And now she's missing some tools that she stored out there." He paused, then added in a serious tone, "They belonged to her late husband."

April's humor disappeared at the allegation leveled against the teen Colton had taken under his wing. Initially, he'd been against having a boy from the juvenile corrections facility working for them. But after he'd come to know Steven, he came to see he'd been wrong in assuming the worst about him.

"Steven works hard here," she said. "He doesn't have the time or the desire to get into trouble."

The boy *had* been on that section of the camp-ground property yesterday, repairing loose boards and pounding nails that had worked their way out of the salt-treated wood fence. But April had no doubt that he'd stayed on campground property. He was trying hard to prove himself to Colton. The teen wouldn't throw it away by doing something as foolish as what the deputy was implying.

Colton straightened the tall brown hat that often served as an indicator of his moods. Today, perched menacingly low over his scowling brow, it sent a clear warning. He frowned at Dugg.

"Are you here to press charges?"

"No, no," Dugg insisted, waving his hands. "There isn't enough evidence. But I *am* here to issue a warning. Perhaps you could hint to the boy that if those tools are mysteriously returned to Mrs. Turner—undamaged—then we'll forget about the whole incident. Provided, of course, no other items disappear from her property in the future."

April was about to tell him what he could do with those tools, but Colton placed a firm hand on her shoulder. When she opened her mouth to speak, he quelled her protest with a slight shake of his head.

She supposed he was right. Dugg's citation pad had stayed in his pocket on this particular visit. If she started arguing with him now, he'd surely charge them with some infraction—real or imagined—that he could think of on the spot.

Colton turned to go inside and paused at the door to the building that served as a combination camp store and recreation room.

"We'll mention to Steven about Mrs. Turner's missing tools, but I'm certain he doesn't know anything about them." Holding the door for April, he added, more for Dugg's ears than hers, "There's too much work to do for us to be standing around out here."

Without so much as a word of goodbye, he ushered her inside and followed with a firm click of the door. To their surprise, the bell above the door tinkled again as it swung open and their nemesis stepped inside.

Clyde, their part-time employee, wheeled his chair out from the aisle where he'd been stocking pool toys in preparation for the summer guests. When he saw who was with them, he reversed the direction of his wheelchair.

"Is there something else?" Colton delivered the words more as a statement of dismissal than a question.

The deputy paced down the aisle where Clyde was now loading shelves with plastic snorkels and inflatable pool toys. He examined the procedure as if he were about to give the elderly gentleman a performance review.

Turning back to Colton, he asked, "Got any cold drinks?"

Colton's hat brim nodded toward the refrigerated compartment along the back wall where large red lettering above it spelled out COLD DRINKS.

The deputy went to the cooler, retrieved an orange soda, and downed half of it before he reached into his pocket to pay for it. He was headed toward the cash register when he abruptly stopped, peered through the refrigerator's glass doors, and studied the neat rows of bottles, cans, and cartons. The pink-faced man grinned as if he'd single-handedly tracked and apprehended one of America's most wanted criminals.

Alexander Dugg licked his lips and hitched his breeches a little higher.

"What do we have here?" Dugg asked, reaching once again into the cooler.

April's stomach felt as though it hit the floor. It was clear Colton had also seen the can of beer in Dugg's hand.

From Dugg's smug smile, April supposed he was picturing the headline: *Deputy Busts Campground Owners for Illegal Alcohol Sales*. Perhaps he even imagined that Lisa LaQuinta, the TV news reporter, would interview him. If April knew Dugg as well as she thought, he was probably making a mental note to take his uniform to the cleaners for the occasion. And he'd ask for extra starch. She wouldn't be surprised if he thought such publicity would give him a shot at the sheriff's job in the next election.

The deputy sauntered to the front of the building and placed the can on the counter in front of April. "How much do you charge for this?"

"We don't," April said. Remembering the deputy's eagerness to achieve his self-made quota each weekend, she forced herself to speak with as much caution as she could muster. "We don't sell alcohol here."

"Coulda fooled me." Dugg turned the can over to display the price tag. "Let me see your liquor license."

When Colton stepped forward, Dugg touched the gun at his side as if to reassure himself it was still there.

Apparently noticing the deputy's find, Clyde

rolled his chair toward them and cleared his throat to say something. The expression of guilt on his face made him look, despite his seventy-plus years, like a small boy holding a baseball bat near a broken window.

She should have known. Clyde had often remarked that he slept better at night after "downing a cold one." But she didn't realize he'd been keeping those beers in the camp store's cooler.

Before he could speak, however, Colton silenced him with a slight shake of the head. "That's mine," he told Dugg. "It's for personal use."

To make sure their employee didn't make matters worse by confessing his part in the mix-up, April distracted him by handing him the squirrel to care for. For a moment Clyde looked torn between responsibilities, but ultimately went away to look for a box and bedding for his new charge.

"Personal use, my eye," the deputy argued. "This can has a *price sticker* on it."

Colton's hands moved to his blue-jeaned hips. With his feet slightly apart, ready for confrontation, he reminded April of a cowboy preparing to shoot it out.

"If you'll take a look around," he said, his voice low and steady, "you'll see that we don't sticker any of our drinks. The price list is posted on the cooler door."

Her partner's patience was being tested, perhaps more than her own. It was stupid, having to put up with this kind of harassment, but there came a point when it was senseless to fight over inanities. Maybe if they just took their lumps and made an appropriate apology, the deputy would go away satisfied that he'd won.

"Look," said April, "we have a business to run, and I'm sure you have some other deputying to do. So why don't you just tell us how much we owe, and we can call an end to this misunderstanding."

She pulled her purse out from under the counter. Colton tried to stop her, but it was too late. Her wallet was already open, and she was counting out bills onto the Formica counter. A low moan escaped the back of his throat.

Dugg's eyes widened. "Miz Hanson, you are obviously mistaken about my ethics as a law enforcer."

A quizzical expression crossed her face. "What? I only—"

If he let her say anything else, she was only going to worsen the situation. Colton spoke up, effectively preventing her from digging the hole any deeper. "I believe my partner is trying to say that she would be willing to pay whatever *fine* is involved."

But Dugg wouldn't accept his explanation. "I'm going to have to charge you both with selling beer without a license." He glanced at April. "And attempting to bribe an officer of the law."

She tried to protest but was drowned out as Dugg launched into the Miranda speech. "You have the right to remain silent..." When he finished reading them their rights, he fished a pair of handcuffs out of his back pocket.

Clyde rolled his chair toward them, the squirrel in a cardboard box on his lap, and rubbed the sprinkling of gray whisker stubs on his chin. "Colton, I gotta tell you—"

Colton cut him off. "We need you to stay here and take care of things until we get back. And keep an eye out for Steven. He should be arriving soon."

His message was clear. *Don't say anything else, or there will be three of us going to the sheriff's office.*

"Hold out your wrists," Dugg said to April.

She stared helplessly at the cuffs the little man held out toward her. With a quick, pleading glance at Colton, she slowly lifted her arms.

A knot formed in Colton's gut. There was no way he was going to stand by and let that little twerp handcuff April. His big hand shot out and, without thinking about the consequences, he snatched the metal hardware from the deputy. "Hey!" Dugg yelped. "Give those back."

"You are not going to put these things on her."

"Okay, you've done it now." Dugg hitched his pants up and touched the gun at his side. "I'm going to have to charge you with interfering with an officer of the law in the performance of his duties."

This wasn't Mayberry, and Colton doubted the deputy was required to carry his bullets in his shirt pocket. Since Dugg was already agitated and obviously out of control of the situation, Colton knew it would be foolhardy to back him into a corner.

"Charge me as you see fit," he said, dangling the stainless-steel cuffs from one finger, "but the lady doesn't wear this style of bracelet."

Dugg grabbed the cuffs from Colton and stepped back a pace as though he might get bitten if he ventured too close. "I'm gonna have to ask you to hold out your arms."

April moved beside him, and Colton felt her arm slip around his waist. "You don't need to use those on him," she said. "He's never hurt anyone in his life."

If the deputy hadn't been clamping steel around his right arm, Colton would have smiled at her words. She'd conveniently forgotten about the times he'd defended her from schoolyard bullies and left them with bruises or bloodied noses.

He waited patiently for the circle to close around his left arm, but Dugg said, *"Behind* your back."

"Oh, for crying out loud!" April stepped away as Colton turned to accommodate the deputy.

Their eyes met, and Colton wished he could protect her as easily now as when they were kids.

Order Colton now.

ABOUT THE AUTHORS

Carolyn Greene

On Carolyn Greene's second-grade report card, her teacher commented, "Carolyn writes nice stories." Shortly after that, Carolyn got hit in the head with a kickball which she credits for her ability to take her romance novels and cozy mysteries in unexpected directions. Over the years, she has been nominated for, or won, numerous writing awards.

Carolyn met Lori Wilde through an online writing forum more than twenty years ago, and they immediately bonded over their mutual love of romantic comedy. Since then, they've brainstormed dozens of novels together and shared a close friendship.

Carolyn lives in Virginia with her hot firefighter husband and two amusing miniature pinschers. They have two grown children and two grandchildren who give her plenty to write about.

Lori Wilde

Lori Wilde is the New York Times, USA Today and Publishers' Weekly bestselling author of 87 works of romantic fiction. She's a three time Romance Writers' of America RITA finalist and has four times been nominated for Romantic Times Readers'

Choice Award. She has won numerous other awards as well.

Her books have been translated into 26 languages, with more than four million copies of her books sold worldwide.

Her breakout novel, *The First Love Cookie Club*, has been optioned for a TV movie.

Lori is a registered nurse with a BSN from Texas Christian University. She holds a certificate in forensics, and is also a certified yoga instructor.

A fifth generation Texan, Lori lives with her husband, Bill, in the Cutting Horse Capital of the World; where they run Epiphany Orchards, a writing/creativity retreat for the care and enrichment of the artistic soul.

Southern Charmers

Reece

Blake

Boone

Colton

By Lori Wilde

Texas Rascals Series

Keegan

Matt

Nick

Kurt

Tucker

Kael

Truman

Dan

Rex

Clay

Jonah

Made in the USA
Las Vegas, NV
08 June 2022